The Reviewers Rave About Ed Gorman

HAWK MOON

"[HAWK MOON] is written in a superb racy style . . . The murders are grisly, the solution thrilling [and] the one-liners brilliant."　　　　　　　　　　—*Evening Standard* (UK)

"Solidly written . . . Entertaining."　　　　　　　—*Booklist*

"Gorman's narrative flows smoothly, the writing is lean and characters are sharply etched."　　　—*New Mystery*

"Packed with suspense . . . HAWK MOON offers plenty of surprises in a detective series that will hopefully continue on for many more, ah, moons to come."

　　　　　　　　　　　　　　　　　—*Pirate Writings*

"Ed Gorman excels . . . [He] develops a solid plot with unusual twists and turns that reveal his characters' core. as they demonstrate the underside of human nature."

　　　　　　　　　　　　　　—*Cape Coral Daily Breeze*

BLOOD MOON

"Evocative . . . So suspenseful, so riveting, so involving . . . the characters come fully alive. Books like BLOOD MOON are what inspired me to be a writer in the first place. Steeped in mood yet swift, gripping, thought-provoking, BLOOD MOON really shines."　　　—Dean Koontz

"Crammed with thrills and chills."

　　　　　　　　　　　　　—*San Diego Union-Tribune*

"As much a superb thriller as it is a well-plotted detective story."　　　　　　　　　　　　　—*Mystery News*

"Chilling and gripping . . . another terrific book by this prolific author."　　　　　　　　　—*Cedar Rapids Gazette*

"BLOOD MOON offers the reader a series of well-calculated surprises plus an unusually grueling and suspenseful climax."　　　　　　　　　　　　—*Ellery Queen*

St. Martin's Paperbacks titles
by Ed Gorman

BLOOD MOON
HAWK MOON

HAWK MOON

ED GORMAN

St. Martin's Paperbacks

First published in Great Britain by Headline Book Publishing.

HAWK MOON

Copyright © 1995 by Ed Gorman.
Excerpt from *Harlot's Moon* copyright © 1997 by Ed Gorman.

Library of Congress Catalog Card Number: 95-46782

ISBN: 0-312-96418-8

Printed in the United States of America

St. Martin's Press hardcover edition/May 1996
St. Martin's Paperbacks edition/February 1998

10 9 8 7 6 5 4 3 2 1

To the two best friends a writer ever had—
Rich Chizmar and Kara Tipton

I would like to thank the brilliant Cherokee novelist and poet Robert Conley for reading the manuscript and suggesting key changes in the material dealing with Native Americans; and Bill Pronzini, who also read the manuscript and made several excellent suggestions; and, as always, Larry Segriff for all his work on the various drafts of this novel.

Note: There is no La Costa tribe. Similarly, I have taken some real liberties with Iowa geography.

E.G.

*"If you have not lived through something,
it is not true."*

Kabir—16th Century

1

Barbaric as the practice was, few Indian agents tried to stop it, reasoning that it only proved the general perception of white people that Indians were indeed savages and belonged on reservations.

Professor David Cromwell's Indian Journal

June 3, 1887

Anna Tolan was helping her father shear sheep when she heard the woman's cry on the wind across the cornfield.

Anna looked up, her grip loosening on the sheep.

"Darn it, honey, hold 'im still," her father said.

Anna redoubled her grip on old Henry, the eldest of all the

sheep, as her father used the clippers with quick and nimble skill.

"You hear it, Pa?"

"Hear what?"

"Some woman crying."

"Huh-uh."

"I did. I honest did."

And then the cry came again and this time her father heard it and looked up.

"Be darned," he said. "It is a woman."

"She sounds bad, Pa."

"She sure does."

And with that, he let go of old Henry, who took the opportunity to wobble up on his legs and teeter away to freedom.

Pa stood up, too.

It was a sunny afternoon on the Iowa farm, hogs feeding in the yard, chickens squawking in the shed, milk cows dozing in the barn. Later that afternoon, once he was done with the shearing, Pa would go back to planting.

But now he looked worried.

"Maybe you'd better go inside and help you Ma, Anna," he said.

"Aw, Pa, you said you wouldn't say that anymore after I turned ten, and I'll be ten in two weeks."

He looked down and grinned at her and then swept her up in his arms and kissed her sweet freckled face. "That's what I said, did I?"

"Uh-huh. And you said it at the supper table where Ma heard you and everything."

"Well, then I guess I better keep my word, huh?"

She grinned. "I guess you'd better."

He took her hand and they set off.

Took them half an hour to find the woman. She was on the other side of the cornfield, lying on her belly by the creek.

They could tell right away she was an Indian. The black hair was in braids. The dress and leggings were animal skin.

If she heard them, she gave no sign.

She just kept splashing water on her face with her hands. And sobbing. Of course they couldn't see her face. They were still behind her.

Anna had never heard a person cry like that before. It was frightening.

There were shade trees and sunflowers and cottontails and butterflies here, and it should have been all lazy and beautiful the way things got in the middle of the afternoon.

But there was no way they could be beautiful with her sobbing that way.

Pa signaled for Anna to wait there.

He went up closer to the woman.

Spoke to her.

And that was when she got slowly up and turned around.

And that was when Anna clamped her hands over her eyes.

She could not abide seeing the woman's face.

Covered in blood it was, as were the woman's hands and forearms, all streaming from the dark and bloody hole in the middle of her face.

Somebody had savagely cut off the woman's nose.

"You run back to the farm and be with your Ma now, Anna," Pa said.

She knew that this particular tone of voice brooked no argument. None whatsoever. No amount of pleading or freckle-faced grinning could change Pa's mind when he sounded this way.

Anna stole a last horrified look at the Indian woman's face and then took off running back to the farm and her Ma.

The Indian wars were over now. In Iowa, the various tribes had sold their land to the white government for what amounted to eleven cents an acre. All the tribes were scattered to distant reservations now—all but two, which had insisted on staying in Iowa.

Pa brought the Indian woman back to the house where Ma did what she could for her. Then Ma said they'd better get her into town, into Cedar Rapids, so a doc could fix her up proper-like.

Pa got the buckboard out and took her into town.

When they were gone, Ma made a big glass of cold sugar water for Anna—sugar from cane that Anna had helped cut last fall—and then Ma sat down across the suppertable from her and said, "That was a terrible thing you saw."

"Yes, ma'am, it sure was," Anna said.

"A man has no right to do that to his wife."

"Her husband done that?"

"Indian men do that sometimes, not very often, but sometimes, when they think that the woman—well, when they think that the woman hasn't been virtuous."

Anna guessed she knew what virtuous meant. The priest used the word every Sunday.

"Is she gonna die?"

"No. But he's ruined her life—and that's what he meant to do. She'll always have that hole in the middle of her face."

"I got scared when I saw her."

Ma reached over and took Anna's hand. "You're a good girl, Anna, and I love you so much."

"I'll bet she was pretty, wasn't she?"

"She looked to be."

"And now she won't be pretty no more?"

"Not anymore, Anna, not anymore she won't be."

"Her husband'll go to jail, won't he?"

"Not likely."

"How come?"

"Because she's just an Indian. That's what the Judge'd say. She's just an Indian and it's just Indian business."

"If a white man done that, would he go to jail?"

"If he did it to a white woman."

"I don't see how come her husband shouldn't go to jail, do you?"

"I sure don't."

"It ain't fair."

"It sure ain't, though I asked you not to use that word since you got to the fourth grade and all."

Anna felt scared and alone then and went over and crawled up on her Ma's lap and held her and hugged her the way she did when she was a little girl.

"I feel sorry for her," Anna said.

"So do I," said her mother. "So do I."

Then the day caught up with Anna and she was asleep, damp with sweat and worn with work and worry since seeing the Indian woman cut up that way.

Her mother carried her upstairs to the bed they'd bought her last spring from the old Shaker woman. Her mother knelt next to the bed, holding young Anna's hand, and said a silent prayer that her daughter would never again have to see such a thing.

LA COSTA WOMAN FOUND

NATIVE AMERICAN WOMAN FOUND AFTER SIX DAYS SISTER STILL MISSING

The body of 46-year-old La Costa Indian Sandra Moore was found in an area of deep forest six miles from the La Costa Indian settlement where she grew up.

Police indicate that she had been killed with a sharp instrument, presumably a knife. Preliminary reports indicate that Moore had been dead five or six days.

Local Police Chief Richard Gibbs also responded to early press reports that the victim's nose had been cut off from her face and that her right arm had been severed. "This is in fact what happened but at this point we're not speculating on how or why it was done. We need to see the final report from the County Medical Examiner." Moore's sister Karen is still missing despite continued daily searches for her in and around the settlement and around the apartment house where she lived in Cedar Rapids. Sandra is survived by her daughter, Patricia, who also lives in Cedar Rapids.

The La Costa settlement has been the subject of controversy ever since its gambling casino opened three years ago. While the majority of La Costas are happy with the casino, others cite the Sandra Moore murder as evidence that the crime rate has significantly risen since legalized gambling came to the settlement.

Tribal Leader Jess Conroy argues that the casino has enabled more than twenty tribe members to open their own businesses in and around the settlement—everything from a small grocery store to an insurance agency, Conroy notes—and that the crime rate has *not* risen significantly. "We attract the 'Mom and Pop' type of gamblers," Conroy said. "Not the 'mob' type."

The La Costa tribe has had a long history of difficulties. They were a peaceful group of Plains Indians even before the coming of the whites, the target of several other tribes who wanted their hunting and fishing land. In 1779 more than half the La Costas were killed in a savage three-day war with two other Plains tribes.

The La Costa fared no better with the United States government. Two major treaties were broken by Washington and three times in six years, many young La Costa men died battling the infamous Colonel Daniel Ransom ("The Pride of West Point") whose obsession with destroying the La Costa tribe, historians note, stemmed from the time when he was slapped in front of his men by a young La Costa woman he was trying to embrace.

In this century, the La Costa have lived quietly on their settlement but have suffered from critical unemployment, chronic bad health and an adjoining white community that has never completely accepted them.

It was in this setting that the Moore sisters, Sandra and Karen, grew up. Now Sandra is dead and the same fate is feared for her sister. Investigation continues.

ONE

He was scared and I didn't blame him.

His name was Iron Crow and he was a La Costa Indian. He was also eighty-six years old and about to fly in an airplane for the first time in his life. His sister, who was eighty-three, wasn't crazy about the idea of him flying but she'd finally given in.

We had struck a deal, Iron Crow and I. I would take him flying in exchange for him helping me write my piece on how white explorers, traders, and settlers had swept across the Plains in the last century, driving out, among others, the Crows, the Kiowas and the Cheyennes. He was a gifted storyteller and knew many tales.

I was up in this part of Iowa to do a little fishing and

relaxing, staying five miles due east of a river where pike, bass and perch practically waved white flags and begged you to catch them; and only ten miles north of the limestone cliffs where a famous Indian brave, Big Raven, had jumped to his death rather than surrender to the white cavalry officer who had stalked him across four states. I was waiting for Dr. Lawrence Esmond Ph.D., Big Raven's biographer, to meet me here. He was attending a week-long conference in Chicago where he'd planned to stay only two days. But as yet he hadn't been able to get away and I'd be here till he did.

We stood in a field of buffalo grass in an Iowa meadow on a warm October morning, an arc of geese heading southward down the soft blue sky, and a beautiful sleek mahogany roan running the piney hills to the east. On the wind was the scent of autumn smoke and Indian-summer heat.

Iron Crow was old but he was sweet old, almost boyish old, his wrinkled head and stooped body gussied up in a fancy white Stetson with a single eagle feather sticking out of the band. The rest was a blue western shirt and stiff new jeans and decorative moccasins. He was at the age when the adult becomes the child again. The way he eyed my open-cockpit biplane so apprehensively, he might have been a six-year-old getting his first sight of the school bus that would take him far, far away to a land of dragons and other assorted monsters. Around his neck, on a piece of rawhide, he carried a small black crow's feather he'd told me would bring him luck.

Silver Moon, his sister, a woman just as stocky of body and nervous of eye as her brother, clutched his hand and then leaned over and kissed him. They'd both dressed up for this occasion—she was wearing basically the same outfit as Iron Crow except for the tan Stetson and the red shirt—and there was something touching about that. I could see them as little kids on a hardscrabble reservation, and the notion made me happy and sad at the same time.

"He's going to be fine," I said.

"You won't try nothin' fancy?" Silver Moon said.

"Nothin' fancy?"

"I seen you flyin' out here yesterday. All them loops or whatever you call them."

I smiled. "I was just showing off a little. I won't try anything like that with Iron Crow."

"I'm gonna trust you on that," she said. Given all I'd learned about the Native American tribes of Iowa in the past few months, I knew how difficult it was for her to talk about trusting a white man.

"I appreciate that."

Iron Crow smiled, revealing a set of gleaming store-bought teeth. "I just hope I don't wet my pants when we get up there."

Silver Moon, always the kid sister, nudged him with an elbow. "That's what I was thinkin'." She looked at me and shook her head. "Iron Crow's got this bladder problem. You don't want to get him excited or nothin'."

Then she grinned with her own sparkling set of store-boughts. "'Course, sometimes he pees and he ain't excited at all."

"She forgot to get me my diapers," Iron Crow said. "Last time she went to the grocery store, I said over and over, be sure to get me my diapers, and so she comes back home and guess what she forgot to get?"

"Your diapers?"

"Exactly."

I wore my standard Snoopy gear—leather jacket, leather flying helmet, leather gloves and goggles—while Iron Crow wore the jacket I'd asked his sister to bring along. I'd lent him my spare Snoopy helmet, too. With his grinning false teeth and fierce ax of a nose, he looked like Snoopy's grandad.

The plane is a biplane built in 1929 with a completely rebuilt 1953 Fairchild engine and a nice new yellow paint job—the color of the sun covering the cloth and wood that cover the heart and soul of this particular machine. The machine was suddenly a haze of blue smoke. The propeller cleaved the air with the great poetic power that would help lift us up in a few moments. *Oil pressure. Fuel valve. Booster magneto coil.* These words are lost on modern planes, yet they are vital to old barnstormers like this one.

And then we were off, racing down a field of buffalo grass, Iron Crow crying out in exultation and terror.

We stayed airborne for forty minutes. I didn't do any hot-shotting at all. As a boy I'd watched the scratchy, sacred films of my uncle barnstorming in a biplane very much like this one, and I knew from the time of my ninth birthday that I'd been born in the wrong generation. New planes might be bigger and sleeker and faster, but they had none of the old romance. Today, however, I wasn't trying to impress anybody, not even myself. Here was a man who still remembered the days of covered wagons and the corpse of a dead Indian bringing three dollars if you dragged it back to the reservation—and he'd never flown before. And I wanted it to be nice for him. He deserved good memories. God knew, he had plenty of bad ones.

He shouted, he whooped, he pointed, he even tried to stand up a few times. But mostly he just grinned with his store-boughts and let the cool autumn winds carry us along the soft swift currents. Below sprawled hills and cornfields and creeks and red barns and brown-and-white cattle and the small town of Moon Valley, Iowa. From up here, you could see that the artist Grant Wood had gotten it right, after all. Cartoon-ish as some of his paintings looked, they recreated perfectly the swell and swoop and sway of the rolling green countryside that always gave the impression of deep seismic undulation, the way the shadows and shapes and textures of it seemed to change so fast.

The only thing that didn't fit in this graceful painting of the countryside was the casino, a long, sloping building cross-hatched with neon and blaring with loud tinny country and western music. The parking lot was half-full, and this on a weekday morning. On weekends and holidays, traffic was backed up three miles to the highway. Occasionally, they were even bringing in lounge acts from Vegas. I had no doubt that Wayne Newton would someday be out here, shameless in headdress and singing ersatz "Indian" songs. Some of the tribe, Iron Crow included, didn't like the casino, objecting that the place made them too much like the white men who had exploited their own tribesmen all these years—but the casino was bringing new and prosperous life to the reservation, and who could object to that? There was a new health clinic, a new activity center on the reservation, and several houses were planned for La Costas with young families. And while a group of white businessmen managed the casino now, tribal members hoped to take over complete management in five years.

We flew on, easy, steady, safe, Iron Crow concerned only once when the engine sputtered a little.

But most of the time he was positively beatific, a veritable bird, as one with this old open-cockpit barnstormer.

When I told him we needed to go back, he frowned and looked as unhappy as any other little kid might when you told him you were going to take the magic away.

"I didn't wet my pants," Iron Crow smiled at his sister.

"I know," she said. "That was the first thing I looked for."

They both laughed.

Iron Crow was still a little wobbly when we got back to the car, flying in a biplane making some people unsteady on their feet for a time. Two teenagers from the small airport took care of my plane for me. I'd flown over from my place near Iowa City and then rented this Chevrolet for a few days.

On the way back to town, Silver Moon wondered aloud if she might not try a little flying, too.

"You'd be scared, Sis," Iron Crow said in his older-brother tone.

"Bet I wouldn't be," Silver Moon said, taking up the mantle of little sister.

They were in the back seat, at their own choice. Stocky as they were, maybe they felt they needed the extra room.

"So you enjoyed it, Iron Crow?" I said as I drove.

"Very much. Could we go again?"

I noticed that he still hadn't taken his Snoopy helmet off. Apparently he liked wearing it.

"If I'm around here long enough, sure."

"Maybe we could do a roll or two."

I smiled at him in the mirror. "I think we'd better wait a while for that one."

Silver Moon laughed. "I think you've started something here, Robert Payne."

"Maybe I have," I smiled.

And that was when we heard it, the siren of a boxy white ambulance racing down Moon Valley's main street. West, it was headed. Toward the casino.

"Serves them right," Iron Crow said, nodding to the ambulance. Not all the La Costas had been in favor of building the casino. "Goddamn gambling, anyway. It's not right."

"Pardon his French," Silver Moon said.

We drove on for another five minutes, countryside becoming the dusty streets of a small Iowa town, and Iron Crow said, "Oh shoot, I did it, Sis."

"You sure did," she said.

She leaned forward and tapped me on the shoulder with a stubby, insistent finger. "He did it, Mr. Payne. He peed his pants."

"You shouldn't've forgot my diapers, Sis," Iron Crow said. "Did I tell you that, Robert, that she forgot to buy me my diapers?"

I grinned at Silver Moon in the mirror. "Yeah, I guess I do remember you saying something about that, Iron Crow."

Silver Moon grinned back.

TWO

After I dropped Iron Crow and Silver Moon off at the settlement, where they lived in a handsome new house trailer thanks to the money that the casino had started paying each member of the tribe, I walked back to my car in time to see a group of young children doing a ceremonial dance behind the small concrete block building that was their grade school. Casino profits probably accounted for the new roof that was just now being put on. The tar smelled hot and rubbery in the sunlight.

I'd learned just enough La Costa to understand that the ancient dance the boys and girls were doing celebrated the journey of the sun as it helped sustain the men and women of the tribe who built new buffalo-hide teepees before the snows came.

The children sang in strong, proud voices in the dusty schoolyard, symbolizing with the quick, precise movements of their fingers and hands the long distant days when the tribe had lived in round bark lodges called *wickiups*, and when their clothing was made of deerskin, and when their headdress was a tuft of horsehair dyed red and tied in the manner of a scalp lock, with the rest of their heads shaved clean.

They joined hands now and began moving in a circle, singing of autumn and the hunts of winter that lay ahead.

I had just reached my car when I saw—in one of those terrible frozen moments, like a horrific snapshot—the accident that was about to happen.

A girl of perhaps five had run into the asphalt lane angling past the front of the school. She was all flashy brown legs and sudden startled scream. From the opposite direction came a panel truck moving roughly twenty miles per hour. Driver slammed on brakes. Girl froze. Truck skidded. Wouldn't be able to stop in time.

Brown blur—brown of khaki, starched khaki, crisp tan law—enforcement khaki—a female officer who was slender, pretty, Indian. I got all this in a glimpse. But most importantly, she was quick and agile. It was a perfect TV moment, the way she leapt for the little girl, scooped her up like a football, rolled her up tight for protection, and then dove off to the side of the road. Tumbling.

Safe.

The little girl exploded into tears as the officer released her.

Three people, stout with authority and middle-age, came running from the school to snatch up the little girl again. The officer, finished here, started dusting herself off as she walked to her car which happened to be parked next to mine.

"Man," I said. "That was brave as hell."

She glanced at me and just kind of shrugged slender shoulders. She had the face of a sad doll, equally perfect in shape and sorrow. There was erotic intelligence in the brown eyes and lopsided smile.

"I guess I don't take compliments very well," she said. "Anyway, I was just doing what I'm supposed to do. I'm the reservation cop and the little girl lives here."

I wanted to say more but she didn't let me—and clearly didn't want me to—slipping neatly into her car and backing away before I'd even opened my door.

She turned west, back to the drab gray expanse of reservation.

"You see it?"

"Guess I'm not sure what you're talking about."

"The fight."

"Guess I didn't," I said.

He leaned forward. Glanced along the counter to see if any of the waitresses or patrons happened to be Native American. "Two bucks got into it."

"Ah."

"Drunk as all hell."

"That was the ambulance I heard earlier?"

Leaned even closer. "Kicked the living shit out of each other. I didn't see it personally, but a couple of the guys in the casino said it was one hell of a fight. He says they went ten minutes. Blood all over the place. One of them's in a coma. That's what the ambulance was for."

"I see."

A smirk. "Guess those bucks still know how to fight, huh?"

"Guess they do."

As a former FBI agent—I worked for six years as a psychological profiler back when nobody, not even many of the people in the Bureau, knew what it was—I was not exactly a political liberal. But I didn't like the way this city man with his cheap dusty suit and gravy-flecked tie talked about the Indians here. He might have been handling feces, there was such displeasure in his voice.

"Had a brother lived up here after he got out of the service," the man went on. The half-whisper again. "Said they were the laziest, dumbest bastards he'd ever seen." He shook his head. "Said they couldn't handle their liquor worth a damn, either. That's not a cliché, you know—about Indians and liquor, I mean. They can't handle it for beans." Shook his head. "No, sir. Not for beans. I come up here maybe twice a month to play a little blackjack and I always see a couple of bucks gettin' into it with each other. Just the way they are, I guess. Poor bastards probably can't even help it."

There were a lot of white people in these parts who thought like this man; people who begrudged the little our government gave the Indians after we had slaughtered them and put them on reservations. Not that the Indians were perfect. Some had certainly been killers and savages; and some of them who lived on reservations today were thieves and thugs and murderers. But reservation life was not easy and a whole lot of white folks didn't seem to understand that—maybe on purpose. On reservations, unemployment tended to run up to forty per cent and few teenagers got an education beyond high school. Indian males were three times more likely to die of cirrhosis than white males. And the suicide rate among teenagers on some reservations approached fifteen per cent. The incidence of addiction to liquor and hard drugs was depressing. I knew all this because of the book I was writing, the one I'd promised my wife I'd get around to and never did. Not while she was alive, anyway.

I had an egg-salad sandwich and a glass of iced tea for lunch. I also had a new pal on the stool next to me. Leatherstocking had taken off in search of casino riches. My new buddy wore a green John Deere cap and wanted to talk about last week's murder in town here.

"Cut her nose off."

"That's what I heard," I said.

"The Indians used to do that."

"I know."

"So did the Egyptians. Long time ago, I mean."

"Uh-huh."

I had been going to treat myself to a slice of apple pie with maybe a scoop of vanilla ice cream on the side but somehow the conversation killed my appetite. I wanted to be back up in my old biplane watching Iron Crow in his Snoopy helmet grinning his ass off.

I decided I must have unwittingly taken the unlucky stool at the counter. The one where people didn't let you eat your egg-salad sandwich in peace. The one where people wanted to talk about the most depressing things they could think of.

With my luck, the next guy who sat down would want to tell me how Attila the Hun had once slaughtered more than 3,000 children in a single afternoon.

I paid my bill and left.

What you have to remember about the Indians is that they saw their own kind slaughtered to a degree that is unthinkable in most cultures. At Sand Creek, for example, the US Army, in less than thirty minutes, killed 123 Indians—of whom (according to one observer) 98 were women and children.

Professor David Cromwell's Indian Journal

May 7, 1903

Just about the entire Cedar Rapids Police Department—all twenty-one members—turned up at the murder scene that night.

The reason was simple enough. Cedar Rapids didn't get that many murders, and rarely one as savage as this.

Her name had been Rain Tree and she had been twenty years old and she had been quite beautiful as young Indian women went. Had been. After stabbing her three times in the chest, once directly in the heart, her killer had then cut off her nose.

Anna Tolan had been spending a quiet night at Mrs. Goldman's boarding house, reading a new book she'd ordered on "scientific detection." Though everybody on the force laughed about all the books she read on the subject, Anna believed that in this century pioneers such as the French rogue-turned-detective named Vidocq, Sir Edmund Henderson of Scotland Yard and Alan Pinkerton of the United States would all be proved correct—that murderers could be brought to justice through scientific means. Oh yes, and there was one other, perhaps the most important of all: a Frenchman named Marie-François Goron, who had dubbed his new science "Criminology."

Only Mrs. Goldman encouraged Anna. Mrs. Goldman's husband had been a high-school teacher and an educated man before his untimely death six years earlier . . . and so Mrs. Goldman was open to exciting new scientific concepts. As she always said, "Just walk down the streets of Cedar Rapids and look around. Electric lights and telephones and motorcycles and electric streetcars—who could have predicted these things?"

After the death of her parents in a terrible flood, Anna had moved to Cedar Rapids and gone to live in Mrs. Goldman's boarding house. The stylish, sixty-ish woman became a second mother to Anna, helping her through the worst of the ridicule and scorn when she decided to become a police officer, something many people in Cedar Rapids, including several fundamentalist ministers, publicly and angrily criticized. Mrs. Goldman had also introduced Anna to the women's movement. Anna now spoke openly of a woman's right to vote.

Anna, too, went to the murder scene that night.

The body was found near the Lymington brick factory on a leg of the Cedar River. Lanterns lit the scene now. More than 200 citizens stood around the periphery of the scene, gawking.

The Cedar Rapids constable's uniform consisted of a blue double-breasted jacket, matching trousers, black high-laced shoes, and a hat modeled on the French *képi*. Half a dozen men dressed thus moved about the murder scene now. A sheet had been thrown over the corpse. By now, the sheet was badly stained with blood.

Anna made her way through the onlookers and walked up

to Chief Ryan. As usual, he smiled when he saw her. His only daughter had drowned when she was eleven. It was said that slight, pretty Anna Tolan was his substitute daughter.

Anna wore corduroy pants, a white sweater and a blue jacket. From her right hand hung a large burlap bag that some mistook as an ugly purse. It wasn't.

Chief Ryan recognized the bag for what it was immediately. "Better wait till they get through doing their own kind of work, Anna. Then you can go to it."

"No eyewitnesses?"

"None so far. But you know how it is. Somebody may wander in later tonight."

"Do we know anything about the girl?"

The Chief shook his white-haired head. "Not much. A few people said they saw her in town shopping from time to time but that's about all."

Anna was already getting stares from the other officers. They looked at what she did—her methodical investigation of the crime scene—as something akin to voodoo.

The Chief said, "How'd you like that new moving picture at the Nickelodeon, when that fella goes over the falls in the barrel?"

"You wouldn't be trying to find out if I had another date with Trace Wydmore, would you?"

"Well, I guess my wife sort of did ask me at supper tonight. How things were going with you and Trace, I mean."

She would have smiled but somehow that didn't seem appropriate with the bloody body of a murdered girl only a few yards away. "Let's just say they're going at their own pace."

"He'd make a fine husband."

"Yes, he would.

The Wydmores were Cedar Rapids' most prominent family, instrumental in building the opera house that was the largest and most sumptuous outside of Chicago; responsible too for bringing the best architects, doctors, educators and craftsmen here. And Trace Wydmore, second eldest of the new generation of Wydmores, had been almost painfully in love with Anna for more than five years.

"Well, you keep me posted."
"I will," Anna said. "I promise."

Three hours later, the lanterns died like summernight fireflies, and the body was taken away by a horse-drawn wagon belonging to a funeral home—the clip-clop of hooves sounding lonely on the midnight air. Anna was left alone with her tiny lantern and her large burlap satchel, inside of which she had all the things she required for a "criminological" (gosh, but she loved the sound of that word!) examination of the crime scene.

Anna did not return to Mrs. Goldman's until dawn shone coral in the sky above the Cedar River.

THREE

A casino is not unlike a submarine in that it's a very artificial environment that makes you lose all sense of time and weather.

I am in no way a gambler. Back in the days when I was training to be an FBI agent, I generally passed up the poker games to read a Rex Stout or watch a "Mary Tyler Moore" rerun. When I was still a teenager I had an uncle who lost his car, his house and finally his wife to gambling. He ended up the loudest and saddest drunk at all the family reunions. I couldn't even play Go Fish with my nieces and nephews without thinking of Uncle Bob.

And yet this afternoon, first at the slot machines and then at keno and finally at the blackjack table, I spent more than six hours and $350 proving that I really was not a good—successful—gambler at all.

Not that anybody noticed.

Farmers, college students, local merchants, housewives, blue-haired ladies and bald-headed men on bus tours, cold-eyed professional gamblers, factory workers, schoolteachers, nurses, off-duty cops—they all had their own gambling problems to worry about in a casino that never closed and never quit offering the promise of big quick money for those stupid enough to believe it. This was the place the James Gang had always dreamed of. Whenever the Pinkertons got too close, Jesse and Frank James often elected to scoot across the Missouri border into Iowa, lay low for a time. The only trouble, Frank always lamented, was that there was no place in Iowa worth robbing. If only they could have seen this casino—vast, bright, noisy, packed, soulless as a politician and bursting with enough greenbacks to bribe a Pentagon general.

People talked, laughed, belched, coughed, cursed and sang along with all the country and western songs about heartbreak and deceit. People smiled, frowned, winked, grimaced, teared up and rolled their eyes. People ate tacos, hot dogs, ham sandwiches, pizza slices and egg rolls. People wore orange shirts and green pants and red socks and yellow neckties and pink eyeshadow and black eyes.

And in the course of it, the entire six-hour course, I developed a vague tolerance of, if not downright excitement about, gambling. Only when I went into the men's room to take out my bladder and slam it against the wall—after seven Diet Pepsis such drastic measures are required—did I realize what time it was. And realize what I'd done: lost $350. This was the guy who'd always put at least half his schoolboy paper-route money in the bank. Frugal, some said. Cheap was the word some others preferred. *$350!*

On the floor again, I made a few melancholy passes at the keno and blackjack set-ups but forced myself to withdraw as I felt my hand slipping toward my wallet. The dealers all seemed to watch me with knowing amusement. We just made another convert, their flashing dark eyes seemed to say. I say dark because most of the dealers were Indians. With the prosperity of the casino, the reservation unemployment rate had slipped from forty-two per cent to twelve per cent. Most of the jobs paid $6.50 per hour and provided some reasonably good benefits. If you went to gambling school and learned to deal blackjack or house poker, you could make even more.

I wanted out, then, a sudden animal need for the smell and feel of fresh warm Iowa air, an escape from this submarine of frantic human pleasure and small dashed dreams. On the way out, I passed a shiny red Corvette that you could buy tickets on. But the people who usually won already had shiny red Corvettes, or the money to buy them. God bless the child who's got his own.

On the night air you could smell autumn coming—the heady scent of burning leaves in the hills to the west, the clear clean smell of creekwater to the east, and the slight tang of grass and apples and cornfields as the summer gently burned into fall. I stood on the edge of the back lot overlooking a deep ravine whose shadows almost entirely consumed the neon splashes of the casino.

And then I heard it, even above the country and western music. I heard it and mistook it for something else. And then I heard it again and knew just what it was.

I turned quickly, scanned the parking lot, saw nothing.

The sound came again—a fist driving deep into a man's torso. And the man exhaling pain, and maybe a little blood.

Fear is always my first response. But I was trained to deal with the fear, stay operative as it were, and so I started walking quickly up and down the parking lot.

Looking. Scarching.

On the other side of a horse-trailer that smelled sweetly of hay and horseshit, I found them. Three of them, two doing the hitting, one taking the punishment.

"Hey!" I said.

And one of the men looked up.

He was big and slick—with a cute little gold chain on his fat peasant neck, fashionably ragged crew cut, and the attitude of a man who is both tough and important. When he saw me, he said, "This is our business, Sport."

"Leave him alone."

His friend hit the man again and this time the victim's face swung toward me and I saw it briefly in the lights of the parking lot.

He was Indian. White shirt. Black slacks. Nice-looking—or he would be once he wiped the blood from his face. Young, too, no more than twenty-five or thereabouts. He'd been dealing blackjack while I was losing my money a little earlier.

The man hit him again.

There wasn't much I could do bare-handed. In the days of my FBI training, I'd done passing fair on self-defense, but not well enough that I could effectively take on a bruiser and his smaller but very angry friend. I did the only thing I could do. I reached inside my sports jacket and brought out my Ruger and put it directly in front of the bruiser's face.

I wanted him to be scared and reverent as all hell about the Ruger. He didn't give me the satisfaction.

"Hey, who the hell are you supposed to be, Sport?" he said.

"The Lone Ranger. Now you two walk out here with your hands up. Just the way they do it in the movies."

By now, I'd gotten his friend's attention. He'd stopped slamming punches into the Indian's mid-section.

"He a cop?" the smaller man asked the bruiser.

"He seems to think he is," the bruiser said. "Probably a parking-lot attendant."

The friend nodded at a dazzling black Jaguar sedan. "All right if I go over there and get a rag for my knuckles? I cut them pretty badly."

"Poor baby," I said.

They weren't used to taking orders, either one of them. Even facing a gun, their body language and their sneers said that they were superior to me—whoever I happened to be—and that soon enough they'd be in control again.

"Now what the hell's going on here?" I said.

"None of this is your business," the bruiser said.

"You better have a permit for that, asshole," the smaller man said. In the parking-lot lights, I could see that he was small, slender with the kind of steel carriage, premature gray hair and icy blue gaze I've always associated with successful public figures. Politicians or generals, I suppose. The funny thing was, he'd kept his blue suitcoat on the entire time he'd been beating the Indian. He didn't want to set a bad example by dressing down, not even for assaulting somebody.

That's when the Indian stood up. He'd been leaning against the car, gathering himself, alternately cursing and sobbing.

Now he walked toward us, gave the bruiser a violent shove, and then pushed on toward the lights and noise of the casino.

"You stay the hell away from us, Rhodes, you understand?" the bruiser said.

A few customers spotted the Indian and gave him a wide berth. With the blood all over his face, he looked kind of spooky. He'd also be needing a new white shirt.

"I better not ever catch that bastard poking around in my business again," the bruiser said.

"Or mine," his friend added.

"Whatever he did," I said, "he didn't have that coming. Not two-on-one."

"You gonna kill us or talk us to death, Sport?" the bruiser said.

The temptation was to slam him across the jaw with the butt of my Ruger. But my training was too deeply instilled. Self-restraint was what they taught you at the FBI Academy. In some ways, all good law-enforcement principles depend on self-restraint.

I put the Ruger away. With the victim running off like that, there was no one to press charges, and no reason to call the cops.

The bruiser started for me but his friend put a hand on his arm and said, "Let's go in and find the girls."

"You better be a cop, Sport, that's all I've got to say," the bruiser said.

The friend glowered at me and then led his pal back to the

casino. As they passed me they smelled of sweat and expensive after-shave.

When they were gone, I walked over to the Jag and took out my penlight and played it across the license plate. I noted the number in my pocket-sized notebook; I wasn't sure why. Maybe at some point their license-plate number would be useful.

I walked around to the front and shone my penlight across the steering column. Sometimes people adhere their car registration there. Sometimes. But not this time.

Then I checked my watch and realized it was time to pay a visit to my anonymous admirer at the police station.

FOUR

Mr. Payne:

I'd appreciate it if
you could meet me at
the police station
tonight at 8:00 P.M. Concerning a case.

Officer Rhodes

The note had been left in an envelope angled into my motel-room door this morning. I carried it with me as I walked into the station a few minutes before eight.

There was a front desk, empty, and a hallway, dark, that led to a rear room where a two-way radio squawked and some human voices could be heard. The hall smelled of cleaning solvent and cigarette smoke.

A young chunky guy in a wrinkled khaki uniform sat in front of the two-way console. He might have been a small-town disk jockey running his own board. He had an angular face that did not hide its fleshiness very well, and the kind of haircut you got back in the early sixties before barbers had ever heard of hair-styling.

"Help you?" He didn't sound especially happy to see me. I got the sense that he might have held the playground bully franchise at a very tender age.

"I'm looking for Officer Rhodes."

An unpleasant grin. " 'Officer,' huh?" On top of his radio console was a cup sitting on a saucer. On the edges of the saucer were two donuts. One would have looked inviting. Two looked somewhat obscene.

"Is there an Officer Rhodes?"

"Yeah. Except she doesn't get called that very often."

"What does she get called?"

Looking me over, he lost some of his confidence, unsure who I was, or how important I might be. "She supposed to be here tonight or something?"

"Eight o'clock."

He glanced at a big dusty clock on the wall. It made me think of public school and seventh grade and watching the clock on warm autumn days, ready to shoot spring-loaded from class the moment big and little hands met on 3:00.

"She's got an office down the hall. Guess you could try that. Sometimes she comes in the back door. You know how they are." Then he had some kind of vision and he said, "Hey, shit, I'll bet I know who you are!"

"Oh?" By "they," I guessed that my Officer Rhodes was likely an Indian.

"The serial-killer guy. FBI."

"Something like that."

He shook his head. "Goddamn her, anyway. Chief Gibbs

told her to keep her nose out of it and now look.''

His two-way console crackled into life and he bent his unpleasant face to the microphone. He started doing some fancy
button-flipping with pudgy white fingers.

He glanced up longingly at the donut he'd had to put back
on the saucer.

''Thanks for coming.''

''My pleasure.''

''I was going to introduce myself earlier today but I was
kind of embarrassed about the whole thing.''

''You saved that little girl's life.''

''I don't think he was going fast enough to kill her.''

''Still. You jumped in.''

She smiled. ''I heard you talking to Clarence up there. He
probably told you some stuff about me, didn't he?''

''Well . . .''

''He doesn't like Indians much.'' She grinned again. ''In
a previous life, he rode with General Custer.''

Her crisp good looks and wise erotic eyes were just as
fetching as they had been this morning when she'd flung herself in the path of the car to save the little girl. She wore a
white button-down shirt and a pair of designer jeans. A shiny
badge was pinned to the right front pocket of her jeans. A
standard police Smith & Wesson rode in a small holster attached to the side of her belt.

''I'm Cindy Rhodes. Morning Tree, if you want my Indian
name.''

We shook hands.

''I appreciate you coming over.''

''I always follow down mysterious notes.''

The lunch-room consisted of two tables that looked wobbly, a softly glowing Pepsi machine that resembled an invad-
ing alien, another machine that sold sandwiches and cookies
and candy bars, and a giant-sized Hawkeye poster. Iowans in
this part of the state long ago forsook God and took up the
Hawkeyes. The room needed paint, ventilation and some general cheering up.

"Would you like a Pepsi?"

"You have Diet?"

She assessed me quickly, my rangy body and shaggy blond hair and the altar-boy blue eyes. Bartenders had carded me until I was nearly thirty.

"You don't need Diet."

"Precautionary measure."

"More people should think like you."

I smiled. "I hope not."

She treated me to a Diet Pepsi and then she walked over to a battered door and opened it up.

"This is where the reservation cop has her office," she said.

"They didn't spare any expense, did they?"

"Used to be a storeroom. At least I have a window. And the Chief did buy me this computer."

I had a sense of her as a little girl just then, one completely charmed by a new toy. She was lovelier than ever in that moment, all quick excitement and gleaming eyes.

"By the way, you know Clarence at the radio up front?" she asked me.

"Uh-huh."

"He's the Chief's nephew."

"Oh."

"But it's not what you think. The Chief is pretty nice to Indians. He was raised here and he went to 'Nam with two of my uncles and they got along fine. In fact, the whole generational thing is pretty weird."

"The whole generational thing?"

"Yeah, it's like bigotry skipped a generation or something. The hippie generation got along fine with each other—the whites and the reservation Indians, I mean. But then my generation came along and we don't get along so well. Now it's like it used to be—the way Clarence is, I mean." She grinned her charming grin. "You want the tour?"

"I'd love the tour."

"Well, that's a wall and that's a light socket and—"

I laughed.

She went over and opened up the window.

The night came rushing in, a tide of fading heat and star-light and fireflies and the faint laughter of children and the booming radios of teenagers as they drove up and down the main street.

Her office contained a small wooden desk atop of which sat a sassy new computer. There was a chair that matched the desk and a chair that didn't match the desk. That was the one I sat down in. I faced two battered filing cabinets.

She came over and sat down and turned on her computer. "Have you figured out why I wanted you to come over here tonight?" she asked.

"I've got a pretty good guess."

"Sandra Moore."

"The one who was killed and had her nose mutilated?" I said.

"Right. I want to find out who killed her."

"I guess that's your job," I said quietly.

"I don't mean just because I'm a cop."

"Oh?"

"No. A lot of people in this town think my husband did it."

And for the first time I made the connection I should have made much earlier. A small town; Native Americans. How many people named Rhodes could there be? The bruiser had called the Indian he'd been whumping on "Rhodes."

And the fetching woman sitting across from me was named Rhodes. So that meant—

Never let it be said that the obvious ever slips past me.

"Does your husband deal blackjack in the casino?"

"Yes. Why?"

"He had some trouble tonight."

"What kind of trouble?"

I saw the quick panic in her eyes and was sorry I'd said anything. "He's all right now, I reassured her. "A couple of unfriendly guys from Cedar Rapids worked him over some."

"Do you know why?"

"No. They said he was 'nosing around in their business.'

I'm not sure what they were talking about. I wanted to speak to your husband but he went right back to work."

She sighed, stared out the window for half a minute or so. "I guess I shouldn't call him my husband." She turned back to me. All the luster was gone from her eyes. "We haven't lived together for three or four years. Ever since my second miscarriage." She glanced down at her small brown hands. "That was the funny thing. Women are the ones who are supposed to take miscarriages so hard. And I did. I even ended up seeing a shrink over in Iowa City. But David . . . he really took it hard. That's when he started drinking and running around—" She stopped. And suddenly the grin was back and so was at least some of the luster in her eyes. "But now I'm using you as a shrink, aren't I?"

"I don't mind."

"I'll bet you don't. You seem like a very decent guy, you know that?" She assessed me again the way she had earlier, except this time she seemed more interested in my soul than my body. "But you seem sort of sad, too, you know?"

"My wife died."

"Oh, God. I'm sorry. When?"

"Couple of years ago."

"Cancer?"

"Brain aneurism. We were standing in the kitchen just talking and—"

"I really am sorry."

I smiled. "Now I'm using you as a shrink."

"Well, I'll say what you said to me—I don't mind."

We looked at each other a long moment and then she said, "I guess we probably should talk about the murder, huh?"

"Probably be a good idea."

"Where should we start?"

"Why don't we start by you telling me why some people think your husband killed that woman?"

"Yeah, I guess that would make sense, wouldn't it?"

Only the black male was held in lower regard than the Indian man. Invariably, when a local white was mur-

dered, and there were no handy suspects, Indian males
were questioned by police.
                    Professor David Cromwell's Indian Journal

May 12, 1903

Chief Ryan didn't want to create a scene—it was just after
suppertime and the potential for a crowd of onlookers was
great—so he went over to the livery stable alone. He wore
street clothes, his five-pointed badge on the breast pocket of
his Edwardian-cut jacket, and he carried his old Remington
.36, which he'd had altered so it could use metal cartridges
instead of the original paper ones.

The way he figured things, there wouldn't be much trouble.

The young Indian man he suspected of killing the Indian
girl the other night had a room above the livery and was said
to be there right after suppertime most nights. He was also
said to have argued violently and publicly with the girl on
the afternoon of her death. And he had an extremely bad
drinking problem. Ryan felt sure he had his man. Now it was
simply a matter of arresting him, hopefully without incident.

After supper, Anna Tolan went back to the crime scene. She
wanted to comb a particular area of grass once more before
the rain came and washed all the evidence away.

She spent half an hour at the scene and then walked back
toward town.

As a farm girl, she was always properly thrilled by Cedar
Rapids. Nearly 30,000 population now, electric lights, more
than 2,000 telephones, electric trolleys and theaters that saw
some of the world's biggest acts play here. She loved win-
dow-shopping, too, especially since the large floral hats were
in for spring. She was saving her money up to buy one.

Even from the back, she recognized him. Chief Ryan.
Walking fast. Alone.

She caught up with him. "Good evening, Chief."

"Hi, Anna." But he didn't sound as hearty as usual. In
fact, he didn't sound all that happy to see her.

She walked along with him. In silence. "Everything all right, Chief?"

"There could be a little trouble, Anna."

"Oh?"

"The Indian girl."

"Uh-huh?"

"I think we've got our man: I'm just going to arrest him now. I don't think it's any place for you, Anna, and please don't take that the wrong way."

"I have my own gun."

"I know you do."

"And I'm a good shot."

"I know you are."

"So I'm perfectly capable of taking care of myself." Mrs. Goldman, who was educated, always said things like "perfectly capable," and Anna loved the sound of such words in her ear and the feel of them on her very own tongue.

The Chief sighed. "So in other words, you want to go along."

Anna nodded. "Yes, I do. But I should tell you one thing."

"Oh?"

"I don't think he did it."

"You don't, eh? Is this more of your 'scientific detection?' "

"Uh-huh."

"Well, now's not the time for it, Anna. We've got our man and we've got him good so if you want to go along with me to arrest him, can you please just be quiet about your scientific detection for once?"

Anna said, "I'm perfectly capable of being quiet when I need to be, Chief."

FIVE

I'll tell you a secret about sexual homicides: the stranger the better where the FBI's psychological-profile group in Quantico, Virginia is concerned.

There's a good reason for this. Find a man in an alleyway who has been murdered by a blow with a beer bottle, and your lists of suspect types will be virtually endless. Many different kinds of people are capable of committing a homicide such as this one. The death might even have been justifiable homicide—maybe the killer was a woman fending off a rape.

The case that the Bureau often points to as a seminal one took place in October, 1979. The victim was a white twenty-six-year-old teacher who had been found on the roof of an apartment building. The killer had sliced off her nipples and written *Fuck you. You can't stop me* in ink on the inside of her left thigh.

The nature of the crime narrowed the scope of the investigation immediately and significantly. After studying the crime scene and the Coroner's reports, the three agents working on the case began listing some assumptions about the killer. He would be

* white

* 25–35 years old

* a high-school drop-out

* living by himself (or with a parent)

* intensely interested in pornography

New York homicide detectives took this and all the other data in the profile and began checking the immediate neighborhood where the woman had been murdered.

Three days later, they started interviewing a man who was

* white

* 30 years old

* lived with his father

* had a large collection of pornographic magazines

* lived in the same building as the victim

That's what I mean by the stranger the better where sexual homicides are concerned. The very nature of the atrocity helped focus the investigation. As far back as 1955, the Bureau started keeping extensive records of bizarre murders. By now, they have thousands of detailed profiles of sexual sociopaths. This is coupled with a lot of other information—weather conditions at the time of a murder, the political and social environment, domestic setting, employment, reputation, habits, fears, physical condition, criminal history (if any), family relationships, hobbies, social conduct—and then the autopsy report with toxicology/serology results, autopsy photographs, and photographs of the cleansed wounds. And that's just the opening phase of the investigation.

"I tried to get things ready for you," Cindy said. "I hope I used the right forms and everything."

She handed me a formidable stack of papers from her desk. The top page bore the familiar logo of VICAP (The Violent Criminal Apprehension Program), the standard report used by both the Bureau and an increasing number of law-enforcement departments throughout the country.

"Take a look at Form 8, will you? I'm not sure I filled that out right."

I looked at Form 8 of the report.

"It looks fine," I said. "But why don't you just tell me a little more about it first."

She glanced away out the window again. The temperature had dropped five degrees during the twenty minutes I'd been in here. You could smell rain. There was a hazy glow around the silver quarter-moon.

"We all grew up here, on the settlement, I mean—David and me and the two Moore sisters, although they were quite a bit older than us. They left here when they were still in their teens, I think. They were very, very beautiful and they made their looks their stock in trade."

"Prostitutes?"

"Probably. But not for very long, I don't think. They were more 'kept' women than anything. You know, for rich men. They spent a lot of time in Vegas and then in Los Angeles and then they came back here. Even in their forties they were beauties. They really took care of themselves. But of course

VIII. CAUSE OF DEATH AND/OR TRAUMA

160. Estimated Number of Stab Wounds: __8__

161. Estimated Number of Cutting Wounds: __11__

162. Estimated Number of Gunshot Wounds: __0__

163. Range of Gunfire:

1 ☒ Not Applicable		4 ☐ Close (powder residue / tattoing)
2 ☐ Distant (no stippling / tattooing)		5 ☐ Contact
3 ☐ Intermediate (stippling / tattoing)		

BITE MARKS ON VICTIM

164. Bite Marks Were Identified on the Victim's Body:

1 ☐ Yes 2 ☒ No

165. Location of Bite Marks:

1 ☐ Face	6 ☐ Groin
2 ☐ Neck	7 ☐ Genitalia
3 ☐ Abdomen	8 ☐ Thigh(s)
4 ☐ Breast(s)	9 ☐ Other (specify) _____
5 ☐ Buttocks	

ELEMENTS OF TORTURE OR UNUSUAL ASSAULT

166. There is Evidence to Suggest That the Offender Disfigured the Body of the Victim in Order to Delay or Hinder Identification of the Victim (burned body; removed and took hands, feet, head, etc.):

1 ☒ Yes 2 ☐ No

167. Elements of Unusual or Additional Assault upon Victim:

1 ☐ None	6 ☐ Offender Explored, Probed, or
2 ☐ Victim Whipped	Mutilated Cavities or Wounds
3 ☐ Burns on Victim	of Victim
4 ☐ Victim Run Over by Vehicle	88 ☒ Other (specify) __Nose and 1__
5 ☐ Evidence of Cannibalism / Vampirism	__arm removed__

168. Body Parts Removed by Offender:

1 ☐ None (go to item 170)	10 ☒ Arm(s)
2 ☐ Head	11 ☐ Leg(s)
3 ☐ Scalp	12 ☐ Breast(s)
4 ☐ Face	13 ☐ Nipple(s)
5 ☐ Teeth	14 ☐ Anus
6 ☐ Eye(s)	15 ☐ Genitalia
7 ☐ Ear(s)	16 ☐ Internal Organs
8 ☒ Nose	88 ☐ Other (specify) _____
9 ☐ Hand(s)	

169. Dismemberment Method:

1 ☐ Bitten Off	5 ☐ Sawed Off
2 ☐ Cut – Skilled/Surgical	88 ☐ Other (specify) _____
3 ☒ Cut – Unskilled/Rough-Cut	
4 ☐ Hacked / Chopped Off	

SEXUAL ASSAULT

170. Is There Evidence of an Assault to Any of the Victim's Sexual Organs or Body Cavities?

1 ☐ Yes 2 ☒ No (go to item 178) 3 ☐ Unable to Determine

171. Type Sexual Assault, or Attempt (check all that apply):

1 ☐ Vaginal	88 ☐ Other (Specify) _____
2 ☐ Anal	99 ☐ Unable to Determine
3 ☐ Victim Performed Oral Sex on Offender	
4 ☐ Offender Performed Oral Sex on Victim	

their rich men started wanting younger women nonetheless. And that's when the sisters went into procuring. I know they steered a couple of girls from the settlement into prostitution.''

"And your husband knew them?"

"The sisters lived and worked out of Cedar Rapids and that's where David liked to drink and run around. Over the past few years, he had relationships with both of them, I'm pretty sure."

"Why would he want to kill them?"

She shook her head. "I'm not sure. Just all of a sudden, he became enraged when you just mentioned their names."

"But he never said why?"

"Never."

"He has a drinking problem, doesn't he?"

"Bad one. He's been through detox in Cedar Rapids twice in the past three years."

"Did he ever beat you up?"

"Pushed me around a little, but not beat me up."

"You think he's capable of murdering somebody?"

She hesitated. "I suppose. That's the only way I can answer honestly. Under most circumstances, no. He's a brawler but he's not a killer. But under the right circumstances . . ."

"If he was drinking, you mean."

"Yes, and if he'd been hurt badly enough."

"Hurt?"

"He's one of those rough, tough men who is very vulnerable. He doesn't want to be but he can't help it. He feels betrayed very easily. And if he's been drinking on top of it . . ."

"You have any idea what the sisters could have done to make him hate them so much?"

"Not really. He came over to my place one night real drunk and put his head down on my kitchen table and just started sobbing. I'd never heard him cry like that before. It was really sad and sort of scary, too."

"How so?"

"All the crying—I saw how desperate he was. He was really lost."

"Did he give you any hints about why?"

"Just that he had been going to get married and she broke it off. He was devastated." She sighed, glanced out the window again. "It's funny how you can smell rain coming, isn't it?"

"I was just thinking the same thing."

"I had a dog on the settlement—a teeny tiny puppy. He got lost in a rainstorm one night when I was a little girl. In the morning my father found him drowned in a storm sewer. Even now, when I know it's going to rain, I get scared. I can't help it."

I studied her a moment. I liked her. Ever since my wife died I've come to have a special appreciation of women, their patience, their courage, their gentle wisdom. My wife was like that, too. I just hope I told her enough how much she meant to me.

"You're a damned nice woman, anybody tell you that lately?" I said.

She smiled. "No, I guess not." Then she laughed. "But I guess I wouldn't mind hearing it every now and then."

"Well, somebody should tell you that at least once a day." Her puppy and the miscarriages and loving a husband who was long past loving her—and enduring it all with intelligence and dignity and even some humor. You can keep your movie stars and politicians. It's the brave everyday people who impress me the most. They don't have any agents or consultants to keep them from colliding with reality. They just have to do the best they can by themselves.

But I was getting choked up over my wife again. This was how it usually manifested itself, in a sudden gushy sentimentality that could get sticky if I wasn't careful. So I said, "What does your boss think about the murder?"

"If David killed her or not?"

"Uh-huh."

"He's sure David killed her."

"Why's he so sure?"

She tapped the report that sat on the edge of her desk. "He doesn't believe in any of this. He'll fly off to a crime conference or two every year but basically he thinks the whole scientific approach to crime is just a way of keeping the Washington bureaucrats in big salaries."

"In some cases, he's probably right."

"But in this case, he's wrong. He's sure David did it because David is a drunk and has a bad temper and because he was seen arguing with the sisters several times."

"How about crime-scene evidence? Anything to tie David in there?"

"Unfortunately, yes. There were some cotton-and-polyester fibers found under the fingernails of Sandra Moore's right hand. They match the fibers of the shirt David was wearing that night. The problem is, Sears was having a sale that week and they sold around one hundred shirts just like it."

"So the Chief needs a little more evidence?"

"Yes. And he's getting around to it. He's interviewing a farmer who claims to have seen David near the woods the night Sandra was killed."

"Where was this?"

"There's a block of old retail stores that went out of business ten years ago when the mall came in. That's where she was killed. Behind there. And that's where the woods are."

"Anybody figure out what she was doing there?"

"No. But I think she was probably meeting somebody."

"Any idea who?"

"Not yet."

"Could it have been David?" I said.

"Could have been, I suppose."

"How about David? What's he say about all this?"

"Says he didn't kill her," she said. "And that's *all* he'll say. Even when I scream at him, try to make him see that he's just making everything worse by not cooperating—all he'll say over and over is that he didn't kill her."

"Does he have an alibi for the approximate time of her death?"

Officer Rhodes shook her head. "No. He told the casino boss that he wasn't feeling well and took off early that night." She paused and then said, "I can't afford you."

"I know."

"But if I paid you two hundred dollars, would you look over the reports and give me your assessment?"

"You know how to cook?"

"Not very well. Except for red snapper, I guess. Red snapper I'm pretty good at."

"How about a red-snapper dinner instead of the two hundred dollars?"

"God, I couldn't do that, Mr. Payne."

"Robert."

"I really couldn't, Robert."

"Sure you could."

"I could buy a cake or a pie for dessert, I guess."

"That sounds great."

"You like spinach?"

"Very much."

"The woman upstairs has a nice little garden in the back. She's always after me to take some spinach."

"How about tomorrow night?"

"I still want to pay you something."

"A home-cooked meal and the company of a pretty woman is a very handsome reward, believe me."

Rain affected me the way it did her. I felt lonely now, bereft of my wife, and I wanted to sit in a lamp-lit living room in the comforting presence of a graceful and gracious woman, both of which Cindy Rhodes a.k.a. Morning Tree offered in abundance.

"Here's my address."

I picked up the report she'd given me then stood and walked over to the window.

You could hear the night animals settling in for the summer rain that was just now getting underway, hiding under porches or in the car-smelling darkness of garages, or on backporches if they were cats or dogs and lucky enough to have masters who treated them like human children.

When I turned back to her, she had tears in her eyes. She said quietly, "He didn't kill her, Robert. He really didn't."

On the way out, Clarence looked away from his radio console and gave me a frown. Both of his donuts were gone.

SIX

I drove back to the casino in the rain. All the neons looked like watercolors through the steam on my windshield. Parking spaces were still tough to find. I had to settle for a very tight slot next to a Dumpster. Before going in, I checked on the black Jag. Still there. In the dampness, you could smell all the trees. I wanted to stay outside, even if it meant getting wet.

They were all in there, waiting for me. All the tourists who wanted me to join them in losing some more at the slot machines, all the waitresses who wanted me to ruin my stomach-lining with tacos and hot dogs, and all the dealers who wanted to take my money.

But there was only one dealer I was willing to drop a few bucks with.

David Rhodes didn't seem to recognize me as the man who'd broken up his beating. For just a moment there was a tiny spark of something in the dark eyes but then it vanished.

He took my bet and started dealing the cards. We were alone at the table.

I said, "Why'd those guys want to pound on you tonight, David?"

Except for a slightly puffy left eye, he looked pretty good. New white shirt. New dark slacks. Hair slicked back. An air of anger and hot quick intelligence about him.

"Who are you supposed to be, man?"

"Payne—if it matters. I'm helping Cindy a little."

"Cindy don't run my life."

"She's worried about you."

He grinned and it was an arrogant grin and I realized that I didn't like him at all. This was the guy Cindy had waited all her life for and he smirked when I mentioned her name. A real sweet guy, this one.

"She's been worried about me since we were kids, man. And it hasn't done her much good, has it?"

The smirk was still in place.

Unfortunately, it probably always would be.

He hadn't had money or name or promise to cling to while growing up, so he'd invented himself as a cool street dude. There were millions and millions like him in the inner cities. They played the hard-ass role long enough, they actually became hard asses and convinced themselves, just as they tried to convince you, that nothing meant anything to them, that they'd just as soon kill you as talk to you. There's an old French saying about beware of what you wish for . . . it just might come true. Prisons and Death Rows are filled with guys who just couldn't wait to become heartless punks. I wanted to feel at least a little sorry for him, growing up on the reservation and all, but somehow I couldn't. Not quite.

"How come they hate you so much?"

"That's none of your business. Now, you want to play blackjack or not?"

I nodded.

We went three hands. House won every one of them.

"You have something on them?"

"Why don't you take a hike, man—all right?" But for the first time anxiety was present in his voice. There was something he didn't want me to know, and when I pushed him he got scared. Fear shone in his eyes: I took some satisfaction in putting it there.

"You shaking them down?"

He started dealing another hand.

"Or maybe you're bopping one of their wives."

Rhodes made as if to come at me—right across the table—but then he saw the suit walking about twenty yards away, glad-handing everybody he met.

The suit would undoubtedly be unhappy if he saw one of his blackjack dealers try to punch out one of the paying customers. Suits are funny that way.

"You're gonna pay," he hissed. "Believe me you are. Now get the hell away from me, man."

I hated to think of Cindy Rhodes with this guy. All those years. All that waiting and heartbreak. For him.

He looked as if he wanted to say something more but then a customer came up. He glowered at me and then asked the customer what his pleasure was.

I roamed around for a while. The human noise of it all calmed me down. David Rhodes had been a real disappointment. I'd been under the illusion that maybe I could help Cindy prove that her husband really was the great guy down deep she seemed to think he was. But all I wanted to do was push his face in.

A grandmother won $100 on a slot-machine and gave me a kiss. A hefty guy in a paper cowboy hat demonstrated his prowess as a line dancer just outside the small restaurant. The jukebox was playing "Achy Breaky Heart." And two old nuns, in formal black habits, sat at the Bingo table crossing themselves just seconds before the announcer called out the next number. They were kind of cute.

I was moving toward the front door when I saw them at a keno table: the two guys who'd been beating up David Rhodes in the parking lot. They'd already seen me. Two women, whom I sensed were their wives, stood next to them.

I don't know what I expected—maybe the bruiser would come after me again, or maybe we'd all haul out weapons and have a shootout on the spot, perfect for the local late news tonight—but what I didn't expect was the young-faced gray-haired man in the natty blue suit to come striding across the floor with his hand out.

"Hey, I'm really glad we ran into you," he said. "My name's Perry Heston, by the way. This is Bryce Cook."

Before I had much choice in the matter, he'd seized my hand and was pumping it with the false hearty manner of a politician.

"Bryce, tell our friend here that you're sorry, too."

It was sort of funny, actually. Bryce wasn't too keen on playing pals. He glowered, he sulked, he frowned, he even made something like a snorting noise. But finally he brought his big hand up as if it were being lifted by an invisible crane.

And brought it down to cover mine.

But Bryce here was no idiot.

Sure he'd shake my hand if that was what Perry Heston wanted. But he'd also grind it into a fine white powder in the process.

His hand clamped on to mine.

I winced. I didn't want to give him the satisfaction, of course. I didn't want to wince. I wanted to show him that I was just as tough and crafty as he was. But I wasn't. The pain was singular and astonishing. Finally, thank God, he let go.

And it was then Perry Heston produced, as if she were part of a stage magic set-up, a very beautiful dark-haired woman in a starchy white blouse and designer jeans. "This is my wife, Claire."

We shook. I was tempted to regain my masculinity by

crushing her hand the way Bryce had crushed mine, but maybe she was stronger than she looked and would embarrass me.

I shouldn't have liked her but I did. Beyond the somewhat mannered country club beauty, there seemed to be an actual human being. There was both pain and odd fleeting humor in her cornflower-blue eyes. In her white blouse and blue jeans and black flats, she possessed a casual elegance I found very feminine and sexy. She wore an air of melancholy like a very expensive and subtly sexual perfume.

"Bryce told me what happened. I'm really sorry." She looked quite embarrassed about it all and glanced at her friend, the blonde, for guidance.

The blonde was six foot and not slender in the way of ideal beauty but there was a peasant grace and sensuality to the Nordic features and short white-blonde hair that suggested intelligence, competence and a merry familiarity with the carnal arts.

"David has been pestering our husbands, I'm afraid," the blonde said and put forth her hand. "I'm Evelyn Cook, Bryce's wife."

And speaking of Rhodes, where was he? I'd tried to keep him in view, to see what he was doing the rest of the night. But now he was gone.

It took me half a minute or so but then I spotted him.

He'd found the boss, who was planting a wet kiss on the cheek of an old lady playing one of the slots.

David was animatedly telling his boss something. He touched his stomach and then his throat. Even though I couldn't hear the words, I knew the story: "I'm sick. The flu, maybe. I need to take the rest of the night off."

The boss didn't look happy about it, nor as if he particularly believed it. But he shook his head sorrowfully and then nodded, and shortly afterwards, David left.

I turned back to Perry Heston. "I'm afraid I'm in a little bit of a hurry."

"I didn't want you to get the wrong idea about us, Mr.—. Isn't that funny? I don't even know your name."

I told him my name. "I appreciate the apology." I wanted to get out of there before he had Bryce shake my hand again.

"Nice to meet you," I said to the women.

"Thank you." Claire smiled, still looking painfully embarrassed. She did not once look at her husband.

I excused myself quickly and left, moving fast through the casino in search of David Rhodes.

I didn't find him.

I wondered what was going on. He didn't want me to know what the parking-lot scene had been all about and neither did Perry Heston.

David was probably going to go somewhere I'd find interesting. I wondered where that would be.

I hurried to the parking lot.

He was just pulling out as I reached it, intense-looking behind the wheel of a rusty five-year-old tan Ford.

He didn't see me.

A minute later, I was in my rental Chevrolet and following him down the two-lane asphalt toward the main highway.

SEVEN

There was fog on the highway, twisting smoky serpents that coiled and uncoiled as I followed the narrow curving road toward Cedar Rapids. The rain had stopped. Rhodes was nothing more than tail-lights that occasionally flared when he tamped the brakes.

We drove a long time this way, passing little towns that appeared then vanished in the fog like images out of nightmares. The neon of tumbledown country taverns was comforting now; at least a little bit of humanity had survived this demon-loosed night.

And then we were in Cedar Rapids.

The fog wasn't so thick here. The deeper we got into the city, heading east on First Avenue, the newer the buildings became, the urban-renewal monster gradually getting everything that wouldn't look good in a four-color brochure. A previous mayor had been obsessed with turning the downtown into a business area, and you could see the results of his handiwork now. What had once been wide open streets had now been narrowed and boutiqued, as if everything on each block were of a single piece. There was a certain obstinate pride about it all.

Rhodes didn't even slow down much through the downtown area.

His speed picked up again around Ninth Street, where the magic of downtown was lost on old and weary buildings that the urban-renewal monster probably dreamt of at nights.

By the time he reached Coe College, he was rolling again. He was apparently one of those people who feel that adherence to speed limits is an infringement of all those God-given rights we like to talk about when we've been caught breaking the law.

By Nineteenth Street, the fog snakes had started whispering and winding through the air again. Houses were lost behind the coiling gray reptiles and an unnerving silence had descended on everything.

He turned left.

Fog and darkness blinded me momentarily.

He began to drive fast up and down narrow streets. So fast that I wondered if he hadn't maybe spotted me and was now going to humiliate the hell out of me by getting me lost or smashed up.

I cut down to fog-lights, visibility had got so bad.

And then, somehow, we reached a long stretch of open country, several rolling acres of farmland here on the edge of the city.

And then he was gone, vanished utterly inside the fog.

Bastard.

All I could do was keep driving, hoping to find the tail-lights again.

I rounded a sweeping curve, angled up a climbing hill bordered with pine trees that wore the fog like white rags, and then started down an abrupt incline.

At the bottom of which I saw a ghost-image of red tail-lights. For just a moment—and then it was gone.

I speeded up. I had no choice: I had to find him again.

I drove as sensibly as I could given the conditions.

An oncoming car loomed up out of the fog, its giant head-lights obscene in the gloom, glaring at me with great and hungry menace, and then nothing again. Just the fog—and him somewhere ahead of me.

I went right past him.

All I got was a glimpse of his car door in the fog and then I was 100 yards down the road.

He'd stopped: I wondered why. Maybe he was hoping I'd go right past him and wouldn't see him. He'd cut his lights. He'd have been awful easy to miss.

There was only one way I could find out. I pulled the rental off to the side of the road, grabbed my flashlight, shut off the ignition, cut the lights and got out.

I was standing on a planet I didn't recognize. Shifting mists and screens of fog cut my visibility down to a few feet. My footsteps on the muddy gravel of the roadside were loud in the silent gloom. The humidity was oppressive; a cold sweat had started filling my armpits.

Without quite knowing where I was going, following the angle of the road, I walked maybe five minutes until I came to Rhodes' car. I played my light inside. Empty.

Why would he have stopped the car here? If all he'd wanted to do was lose me, he could have simply turned his vehicle around after I passed, and driven back the way he'd come.

But he'd left the car.

More monster sounds; menacing monster eyes. A van was roaring toward me, fog running off its sleek sides like smoke. Gone in moments. Leaving me again to the fog and the silence.

I walked several yards past Rhodes' car and it was there I

found it. Narrow asphalt driveway. Rural-style mailbox on a pole.

Was this where Rhodes had gone?

I trained my light on the side of the mailbox, looking for a name. There'd been one once, but it had been crudely covered up with spray paint.

Somewhere down the road, maybe twenty yards, a car engine started and headlights came on. More glowing monster eyes.

Whoever it was, was in a hurry, sweeping quickly from the roadside to the road, and hitting thirty miles an hour by the time they came abreast of me.

I had to jump back. Either the driver didn't see me at all or saw me and wanted to hurt me. All I got was a glimpse of a new green Ford with a crumpled passenger fender.

Then the green Ford was one with night and fog; in moments, I couldn't even hear it let alone see it.

I followed the drive, spending the next ten minutes feeling not unlike a child in a nightmare, the realization slowly beginning to dawn that I had no idea where I was or where I was going. The Grimm Brothers would have loved this place. Any kind of creature from hell you could imagine might lurk in this dark, muggy night.

I was one with the fog now. It was so thick I couldn't even see my own body unless I made an effort.

An owl cried out; and then a dog. The dog sounded nearby.

And then in front of me, running at a frightened angle, a doe on sweet spindly legs rushed to the grass on the other side of the drive. Her eyes were trapped momentarily in the beam of my flashlight. I wanted to give her a reassuring hug but knew that would only scare her all the more. She ran on.

I don't know when the house started to take shape in the murk. It was gradual. First I saw the outlines of the roofs and gables, and then, closer, the square tower or campanile if you want to be technical, and finally, even closer, the shape of the balconies and bay windows. I knew enough about architecture to have a sense of what I was seeing: an Italianate-styled Victorian house.

The owl cried again.

The desolation became overwhelming suddenly and I was once again more child than adult. The fog lapped and swirled, and elongated once more into tatters, and then into sinuous shifting snakes. The moon was lost utterly now.

I stepped forward and as I did so, put the flashlight in my left hand. I gave my right hand the responsibility of slipping my Ruger from its holster and making it snug and ready for use in my grip.

The dog barked again and I felt less alone.

Not until I was very close did I notice the charred areas on the stone exterior walls, and then the smashed-out windows.

I went up to one of the mullioned windows, tapped away to remove a shard of glass so it wouldn't cut my knuckles, and angled my flashlight inside.

The place had been gutted.

The walls were coal-black with char; the floor was heaped with debris; the elegant Victorian furniture had been disfigured by flames and smoke. There was no smell of burning, though. Whatever had happened here had happened long ago.

The fog had penetrated the house, too, twisting in and out of the rooms.

I had just pulled my light back when somebody hit me.

It wasn't a good, clean hit—he or she hadn't struck at the most vulnerable spot on the back of my head—but it was strong enough to do the job.

I heard shoe-leather squeak on the grass behind me.

I wanted to turn and see who'd done it, but—

I fought against going out but it was a useless fight. My body simply shut down. Vision first; and then hearing; and then warmth. A terrible chill shuddered through me. And I collapsed to the ground.

I wasn't out long, two or three minutes at most.

My flashlight had fallen a few feet away from me. The beam was still on. It shone in my face. The grass around the face of the flashlight was very green.

And then the dog trotted into the flashlight's beam, a very

pretty Border collie, with something smudged red across her pretty face.

She was friendly.

She came over and started licking my nose and cheeks. Her tongue tickled and I laughed. Ridiculous to laugh in my position but it was funny. She smelled of wet fur and mud and the foggy night. She belonged to somebody. She was too well-kept to be a stray.

I started to sit up. The headache was massive, arcing across the back of my head, up and across and down into my forehead.

They did a hell of a job for missing my most vulnerable area.

The collie came at me for another kiss but I gently touched her face and eased her away.

And that was when I felt something sticky in the palm of my hand. I reached over, picked up the flashlight, aimed it at my palm.

Blood.

That's what she had all over her face.

I reached out to bring her closer but she was playing hard to get now. Apparently miffed that I'd resisted her earlier advances.

She trotted off into the fog.

Blood.

I got up, which wasn't easy, and closed my eyes against the headache sawing through my cranium.

I liked David Rhodes even less than I had before. I was pretty sure he was the one who'd struck me.

And then my friend the Border collie came back, prim and pretty and proud about what she had in her mouth. My mind didn't want to register the reality of what she was carrying. But I saw how she'd managed to smear herself with blood.

The ripped, ragged arm belonged to a Native American female—that much I could tell even from here.

The upper arm was the part that gave me trouble. After all those years studying serial killers, I had convinced myself that the occasional atrocity didn't have much power over me. But I was wrong.

The contrast between the sweet proud dog and the obscenely severed arm carried in her mouth overpowered me for a moment. All I could do was stand in the vast desolate night, the fog enveloping me, and listen to the distant owl hooting his forlorn prairie wisdom.

I reached down and patted the dog on the head.

She was so damned sweet and earnest sitting there. I petted her some more. I didn't want to break her heart by telling her, "See, honey, we humans have these laws we make up, and one of them is that it's in bad taste to walk around with somebody's arm dangling from your mouth."

She dropped the arm.

She wanted more petting and apparently the limb was becoming something of a chore to keep fixed in her jaws.

I played my light on the arm.

A small light-brown birthmark on the inner elbow was the only distinguishing feature. It wasn't easy to see because of the bruise-like decay of the flesh. Several days dead, I presumed. The stench told me that—a high hard sour-egg smell.

The collie got interested again and dipped her head to sniff at the arm.

I picked her up.

This particular piece of evidence needed protection now— from the elements and the collie alike.

There was a garage to the west of the house. I groped for a door and went inside. The fire had left it alone. It smelled of lingering heat.

The collie squirmed and wriggled as if she were enduring great torture.

After a minute, I found what I was looking for—a cardboard box. I left the collie in the garage, closing the door behind me, and took the box back to the arm.

I carefully set the box over the arm. Safe.

The humidity had sweat rolling down my face and chest and arms. The fog wrapped itself around me.

Maybe somewhere in the gutted remains of the house I

would find the body to match the arm. But that was official police business and I was happy to let them take care of it. They could also let the dog out of the garage once the arm was safe as evidence.

I started back down the drive through the fog.

Ten minutes it took to find my car, and another twenty to move slowly along the road until I located the glowing light of a phone booth.

I pulled in, dug some change from my pocket and phoned the Cedar Rapids Police Department. At this point, I had no desire to get involved anymore than I was already. I wanted to talk to Cindy and then to David.

I told the police how to find what they needed and then I got in my car and drove inchingly back to my motel room in the fog.

Indians and blacks received justice in many cases. But when there was controversy, or when the crime was particularly savage, there was, on the part of law enforcement and the bench alike, a certain rush to wrap things up. To be fair, this same standard often applied to poor whites, as well.
                              Professor David Cromwell's Indian Journal

Not until 3:00 A.M. was Tall Tree brought out from his room atop the livery stable.

When Chief Ryan and Anna first knocked on his door, the Indian responded by climbing out his window and scaling the wall so that he could stand on the livery roof, where he proceeded to hold off twenty armed men until he was wounded in the shoulder by a sharpshooter and finally surrendered. He was very intoxicated and belligerent but denied knowing anything about the death of the young Indian woman he'd loved.

Following dinner the next night, Anna and Mrs. Goldman sat at a table in the parlor, Mrs. Goldman's new electric lamp burning fiercely in the shadows. For a time, they discussed the weekly shopping they did together downtown, when wagonloads of fresh produce were brought in from farms surrounding the city, and when all the shops filled their windows with the latest in picture hats and dresses. This Saturday there were to be several sales. Anna had saved two dollars for a new skirt.

Then Anna changed the subject and started talking about Tall Tree.

"He's innocent, Mrs. Goldman, I'm sure of it."

"The Chief won't listen to you?"

Anna shook her head. "Sometimes he will but not this time. He just sees it as open and shut."

"If he's really innocent, Anna, then you'll have to keep pushing the Chief."

She looked fondly at Mrs. Goldman and smiled. "I will. I just hope he doesn't fire me."

Anna sat up late in the parlor, examining the things she'd found while combing the crime scene that night.

1. She'd made some casts of bootprints she'd found. There were several styles. There were no moccasin prints.

2. She'd found three buttons—two belonged to an expensive male vest; one to a woman's dress.

3. She'd found a tortoiseshell comb that fashionable ladies wore in their hair these days. The comb might have belonged to the victim.

4. She'd found a scrap of paper torn in half. The remaining letters were
ay
ouse
She had no idea what this meant.

5. She'd snuck into the funeral parlor and taken a look at the dead girl's wounds. The killer must have stood too close to her to get much sweeping force because the wounds were curiously shallow, even the fatal one in the heart.

6. She'd found three different sets of ladies' shoeprints but had run out of material for casting.

7. She'd found a strange fishing lure—one in the shape and color of a black moon.

8. She'd found a cravat stickpin that was gold-painted.

She was frustrated that none of these things pointed her in any particular direction.

What good was "scientific detection" if it didn't offer you a road map?

Mrs. Goldman, regal in her rustling robe, came down just after midnight and woke Anna from sleeping at the parlor table.

She helped Anna gather up her crime-scene evidence and then assisted her yawning young boarder up the stairs to bed.

EIGHT

There was somebody in my room.

I walked back to the motel office and went up to the desk, where a fifty-ish woman in a flowered blouse and a beehive hairdo (I think she was doing a one-woman salute to some of the Motown girl groups) read a Janet Dailey novel while occasionally glancing up at Jay Leno through her pink-framed eyeglasses.

"Hi," I said.

She took a long moment to raise her eyes from her book. "Hi."

"There's somebody in my room."

"Somebody?"

"Umm-hmm. A thief or somebody. I wondered if you'd call the police."

She gave me a good, hard look. She was searching, I think, for evidence that I'd been partaking of the grape.

"Why do you think somebody's in your room, Mr. Payne?"

"I heard them."

"They were talking?"

"No. They were knocking things over."

She hooted, then. That was the only word for it. She threw her head back and made a hooting noise.

"That little pecker!"

"What little pecker?"

"Ralph."

"Who's Ralph?"

She set down her Janet Dailey novel, reached over and turned around a small sign that read *Back in a Minute.* "C'mon, hon," she said. "I'll show ya."

Ralph turned out to be a large and not entirely attractive hog who, the motel clerk assured me, was perfectly harmless as long as you didn't leave anything breakable out in your room. Ralph lived in the back, the best friend of the motel owner's eight-year-old daughter. He was an industrious and talented hog, our Ralph. He could climb up on the garbage cans and then shimmy through your window if you'd been silly enough to leave it open. It cost them a lot to replace screens every now and then, but it was worth it for the laugh, and Ralph didn't do it all that often, anyway.

I said goodnight to both Ralph and the lady. The lady was still giggling. Ralph was still grunting.

I did all the things I'd been wanting to do for the past couple hours, including taking a small overdose of aspirin, and then I slipped into bed and slept.

NINE

The knocking on my door seemed to be part of the dream I was having. Two, three times they knocked before I realized it was for real.

I didn't know where I was, not at first. That happens sometimes when I'm on the road. Back in my Bureau days that was a problem. Traveling isn't good for a guy who is a small-town boy at heart.

I tugged on my trousers and stumbled to the door, taking my Ruger with me for company.

There was an eye-hole and I used it.

Cindy Rhodes stared back at me. Her fine-boned face looked kempt and pretty even in the middle of the night. Only the dark eyes revealed something wild and frantic. She'd changed shirts. This one was a blue western-style one, and it fitted her most appealingly.

I opened the door and the hot muggy dark leapt inside like a pet who was supposed to stay outside all night.

"Could we go get some coffee?" Cindy asked me, straight out.

"Sure," I said.

"There's a truckstop not far from here."

"All right."

"This is really shitty of me, waking you up this way."

"You wouldn't do it unless it was important." I smiled and yawned. "At least, I hope you wouldn't."

The truckstop was full of cowboy truck drivers in western shirts and Elvis sideburns and an endless hankering for Hank Williams Jr. records. Sleepy-eyed waitresses transported lots and lots of scalding black coffee to tables and booths. Men came and went from the showers in the back. I couldn't imagine their lives. You hear about the hookers and drugs, but most of these men and women are decent, hardworking folks with families and a real sense of responsibility. The loneliness must get pretty bad: you out there somewhere in Utah in the middle of a midnight blizzard, and your wife and daughter back in Texas dreaming of Daddy in their uneasy slumber.

We had some of the scalding coffee.

Cindy said, "He's in trouble."

"David?"

"Right. Bad trouble."

"I'm not sure what that means." I waited for her to explain.

"Neither am I, but he stopped by tonight and wanted to know how much I had in my savings account."

"Did you tell him?"

"Yes." Pause. "I've never seen him like this—not when he was sober, anyway. Really scared, almost to the point of being crazy."

"He give you any idea of what the trouble might be?"

She shook her head. In the light, her sweet smart face

showed the late hour and the strain. "I'm going to take out two thousand dollars in the morning and give it to him."

"Is that everything you've got?"

"Yes."

"Must have taken you a while to save it."

"He's my husband."

I thought of the way he'd smirked about her earlier at the casino. She was the nice bright girl in the high-school class who always fell in love with the dashing bad boy. Some of those girls never got over those bad boys. Not ever.

"He owes you an explanation."

Sad quick smile. "David's not much on explanations."

I sighed. "David doesn't seem to be much on anything, does he?"

"You don't like him, huh?"

"Let's say I like you a whole lot more."

"He hasn't had an easy life."

"Neither have you."

"His sister. That's how all this started."

"What about his sister?"

"Kidnapped."

"From the reservation?"

"Yes," Cindy said. "She was three years old, playing out in the back yard. Her mom was a good parent, always kept an eye on her kids. But she had to go to Des Moines one day, and had to get a babysitter. And when she got back, her daughter had disappeared."

"Were there ever any leads?"

"Not any good ones. David was obsessed with her. He was one of those brothers who are really protective of their little sisters. He can be very tender. Honest."

The waitress came with more coffee.

"Well," I said, after the lady left, "I feel sorry for him about his sister but he sure as hell hasn't treated you very well."

"I know that, but I want to help him anyway."

"There were two men tonight. They were beating him up,

outside the casino. He tell you anything about that?''

"No. My God, what was that all about?''

"I don't know but it may have something to do with him wanting to leave town.''

I thought of telling her about the burned-out Victorian house and the human arm the Border collie had brought me. David Rhodes had been somewhere in that fog. He was likely the person who'd knocked me out. He was probably in a great deal more trouble than Cindy understood.

"Will you go with me to see him?'' she asked suddenly.

"Now?'' I said.

"Yes. I'd appreciate it. I'm sure he's started drinking and . . . he gets abusive. You know.''

Nope, sometimes they never got over the dashing bad boys. Not ever. And almost no matter what those bad boys did to them, either.

"Sure.''

"This kind of irritates you, doesn't it?''

"Not at all. I almost never have anything better to do at two forty-five in the morning.''

"I'm crazy for still loving him, aren't I?''

I smiled. "Wasn't that the title of the last song they played on the jukebox? 'I'm Crazy for Loving the Dirty Sonofa-bitch'—or something like that?''

She laughed, a burst of pure pleasure that put some luster back into those beautiful dark eyes of hers.

"C'mon,'' I said, "let's go see him before somebody puts more money in the jukebox.''

What was important to know about the relationship be-tween the red and white man was that the red man was perceived as having only four roles in white society— as the wretched drunk; as the lazy reservation Indian; as the impossibly noble icon the liberals contended; or as one of the mainstays of the American criminal class.
Professor David Cromwell's Indian Journal

June 4, 1903

Rain all day, rain all night. Anna had wanted to play basket-ball—she was as good at it as most men—but not in rain like this.

Mrs. Goldman had a bad headcold and went right up to her room after dinner.

Anna stayed in the living room with its elegant twelve-light electric fixture suspended from the ceiling, and its comfortable Victorian furnishings, and its abundance of plants and ferns.

She read the paper, starting with *News in Brief*, which was always her favorite section.

President Theodore Roosevelt declared yesterday that control of the Pacific Ocean must fall under American control in this new century.

More than 100 Jews were murdered in St. Petersburg on Friday of last week.

Professor Albon W. Small, head of the Department of Sociology at Chicago University, predicted at last weekend's Journalist Society that sooner or later Germany and the United States would go to war. He predicted the war will likely come within three years.

William Thompson, of Kearney, Nebraska, will speak at the Cedar Rapids History Society tonight on the subject of scalping. Mr. Thompson claims to have been scalped as a young man and to have photographic evidence of this. A lively discussion is promised.

Anna was still thinking about the last story when she heard the door buzzer. She got up, left the living room and walked to the front door.

"I was just walking by and thought I'd stop in and say hello."

Trace Wydmore. Soaking wet. She knew better than to believe his "just walking by" story. Their relationship had taken a sudden, sharp turn the other night and Anna still felt confused and a little frantic.

She had always considered herself to be a good girl. Now she had her doubts.

Trace, a few years older than Anna, handsome, lanky, shy, came in. Anna built a small fire in the fireplace. Trace sat close to the flames, shivering.

"I really appreciate this, Anna."

They spent a pleasant half-hour, Trace giving her a couple of new facts about the great state of Iowa ("Did you know that Iowa's hens lay eggs that bring an income larger than that of all oranges in the United States? Did you know that the amount paid for Iowa cattle in the stock-market is more than the receipts of all the tobacco crops in the United States?").

"You don't need to thank me anymore, honest."

She was nervous and he was, too. They were going to talk about anything except what they really needed to talk about, which was what had happened the other night.

Trace stared into the fire. "Kind of lonely lately, with my parents gone and all." He raised his eyes and looked at Anna. "Pop says it's time I settle down and take a wife and start a family."

"Sounds like good advice."

"I told you they were in Europe, didn't I?"

She nodded. There was a time she'd been mistrustful of Cedar Rapids' rich people, but in the course of her job she'd met most of them and found them to be, in pretty much the same proportion as not-rich people, good and bad alike.

She was especially enamored of Trace's family. Even though they were always going off to Europe, and always having social events for their friends, they were nice, decent, unpretentious people with a genuine love for this community and its people.

"Say, Anna, did I show you that new keyring I got to give away at the Visitors' Bureau?"

Trace was what you'd call a Booster. There was no subject he liked espousing more than Cedar Rapids. He could have gone into far more profitable work with one of his father's various businesses, but instead he chose to work at the Visitors' Bureau.

He dug in his pocket and took out a keyring and handed it to Anna.

"Shape of a horseshoe, notice that? Supposed to bring you good luck."

"I see that," Anna said, examining the U-shaped key apparatus that was stamped on the curve of the U with: GOOD LUCK FROM CEDAR RAPIDS, IOWA.

Then she noticed the black, moon-shaped fishing lure.

"Where'd you get this, Trace?"

"The lure?"

"Uh-huh."

"From Doug Ashlock back when we started that Semper Fi Fishing and Drinking Club of ours. I guess it was our junior year in college—during the summer, I mean, when we were all back here."

"How many did he give out?"

"Let's see. There were four of us. But what's so interesting about that gosh-darn old lure, anyway? I even forgot I have it most of the time."

"Tell me about the others who got them."

He looked at her, frowning. "You sure you feel all right, Anna?"

"I feel fine, Trace. You have a lure and Doug Ashlock has a lure—and who are the two others?"

"Well, uh, Bob Wethcoat. For one."

"Where is he?"

"Los Angeles. Stocks and bonds."

"Was he here last month?"

"Why, no, Bob hasn't been back here for years."

"Who had the fourth lure?"

"Jimmy Daly."

"And where's he?"

"Dead. Influenza. Remember back in '94? Poor kid."

"So you and Doug are the only two with these lures?"

"Far as I know. I sure wish you'd tell me what you're being so mysterious about."

"How about some hot cocoa?"

"Boy, that sounds great. But I don't mean to put you to any trouble."

"No trouble at all."

"Say, how come you're smiling so much, anyway?"

"Scientific detection."

"Huh?"

"Scientific detection."

"Oh, Lord."

"What?"

"I set you off again. You talk about scientific detection almost as much as I talk about Cedar Rapids."

And then they were both silent and knew that they would have to talk about it now. Not even the things she'd learned about the case tonight could misdirect her attention anymore.

She had to face what she'd done the other night.

And the kind of girl she'd become.

"I don't think we should see each other anymore, Trace."

"God, Anna, what're you talking about?" He looked stunned, shocked.

"We shouldn't have done what we did the other night. And I don't ever want to do it again. I'm supposed to be a good Catholic."

"But that's what people do when they're in love."

"I don't want to be a whore."

"A whore? Anna, a whore! You're crazy! You're a very good girl."

"I wasn't a good girl the other night. I shouldn't have let you do that. And it was my fault as much as yours."

"But I love you and you love me, Anna. That makes it all right, loving each other, I mean."

He came to her suddenly on the divan and tried to put his arms around her but she gently pushed him away.

"All I want to do is kiss you, Anna."

"But then you know what'll happen, Trace—what happened the other night."

It was all so confusing. She had enjoyed the other night so much for that wonderful blinding moment—but ever since, there had been this burden of guilt and shame. When she walked down the street, she imagined that people stared at her disapprovingly, as if they could see what she'd done, see into her very heart and soul.

Harlot.

"It wasn't a home run, Anna."

"It wasn't what?"

"A home run. That's what the fellas call it when—well, when a guy and a gal do the ultimate thing. What we did, well, it wasn't anywhere near a home run."

"It wasn't?"

"No, it wasn't even third base."

"I don't know what that means."

"It's baseball terms, Anna, that's all. First base is a kiss and second base is here," (he pointed to her breasts) "and third base is here," (he pointed vaguely in the direction of her middle) "and a home run is—"

"I see what a home run is. You don't have to say it."

"So all we did was second base. That was all."

Because she was twenty-one years old and because her job forced her to traffic with some very scuzzy lowlifes, some people just automatically assumed that Anna was this really modern type of girl.

But she wasn't.

Not at all.

It had always been Anna's intention to be an absolute virgin on her wedding night.

Oh, a few frivolous kisses with a few frivolous beaux now and then, that was all right.

But not anything else.

"I just don't think we should see each other anymore, Trace."

"Oh God, Anna, don't say that. Please don't. You don't know how that makes me feel. All I'm saying is that if we

do things—just second base and then maybe third base someday, Anna—well, it's our way of proving that we love each
other.''

But Anna was not persuaded.

''You really do need to go now, Trace. Please.''

Trace left.

TEN

Not even the moonlight lent the settlement much beauty. A jumbled collection of ancient mobile homes and shabby little houses, the place spoke of a poverty few white people could understand. The casino's profits hadn't gotten to this section yet.

As Cindy drove slowly through the narrow streets, I saw crumbling cars, rusted lawn furniture and a myriad of windows held together with a myriad pieces of tape.

A tiny, dark mobile home next to the creek was where she finally stopped. "Here."

His tan Ford was there.

"No lights," I said.

"He sits in the dark a lot."

"And drinks?"

"Uh-huh."

"You think he's armed?"

"Hard to tell."

"You mind if I take out my trusty Ruger?"

"Not if you don't mind if I take out my trusty Smith & Wesson. I love him and I want to help him but I don't want to die for him."

I leaned over and gave her a quick but tender kiss on the cheek. "God, I'm glad to hear that."

"The battered-wife stuff getting you down?"

"Yeah, kinda."

"It is pretty pathetic, isn't it, sticking with a guy who beats you up and degrades you all the time."

"At least you've put some limits on what you'll do."

"Dying is one thing I won't do."

"You ready?"

She nodded.

"Let's go," I said.

The air was cool now and I enjoyed it, along with the smell of water and mud from the creek, and the sounds of the night-birds in the trees.

The front steps were wood and they were wobbly.

When we got to the door, Cindy called out: "David, we'd like to talk to you."

She knocked twice, sharply.

"I can't get you that money unless we talk first, David. I'm sorry but it's just got to be that way."

If he was watching us, he saw two people standing on his front porch with guns in their hands. We probably didn't look all that friendly.

The windows were open. Through the screen of the nearest window, a male voice said, "Get rid of him."

"I want him here, David."

"He's an asshole."

"He's helping me."

A snort. "You sleeping with him yet?"

She couldn't hide her pain. "You bastard. You know better than that."

"I need that fucking money."

The booze occasionally got thicker than anger on his tongue.

"Then open the door and we'll talk. All right?"

Night sounds. I looked back across the shanty town of a settlement that inclined downward to a dusty valley. Not much more than a century ago, these people would have been roaming the plains, at one with the birds and the rivers and the steep limestone cliffs.

The door opened up.

He had a gun, too. You could see it in his fist in the moonlight.

It was comic, actually, the three of us standing there with our weapons.

He unlatched the screen door.

We went in.

The trailer smelled of cigarettes, whiskey, heat, dirty dishes and sleep.

He turned on a table lamp, cast in the shape of a bikini'd young lady. I almost wished he hadn't. The furniture was worn and filthy. Pizza cartons with the scabrous remains of various toppings cluttered the coffee table. A pair of dirty socks hung off the arm of the couch.

"God, David, you really should clean this place up."

He smirked. "You wonder why I left you, Cindy? Because of that. Bitch bitch bitch. This place don't bother me, it shouldn't bother you."

He wore jeans but no shirt. He'd tucked his .45 back into his belt. I imagine he thought he looked pretty menacing. All he looked like were half the convicts I'd been forced to deal with in my life. Sad punks, most of them, boy-men who never reached the mental age of twenty-one. Back in 1933 the Barrow Gang—Bonnie and Clyde; if you prefer—hid out in the Iowa town of Dexter. Adults would have kept their whereabouts secret, but Bonnie and Clyde couldn't control themselves at all. Went right on robbing and shooting until they finally brought the law down, a posse of lawmen and angry citizens alike, who surrounded the gang and then killed half of them. Bonnie and Clyde escaped but were killed in another shootout a few months later. Thugs are romantic figures only when they're up on the movie screen.

He sat in a wobbly recliner. We sat on the couch.

She said, "I want you to tell me what kind of trouble you're in."

He didn't say anything. Just glared at her.

I thought of the arm the Border collie had brought me. I said nothing.

"Things got crazy," he said, suddenly.

"What things?"

"What I found out about some of the good people of Cedar Rapids." His face was angry now and he leaned forward. "They put on such a good face for everybody. Such good respectable people."

"David, please, I can't follow any of this."

"No? You can't? Well, too bad, bitch!" He jumped to his feet, swiping downwards with one hand to snag a half-filled quart of Jim Beam.

I just wanted out. And I couldn't believe she didn't want out, too. Some people aren't worth the effort and good old David here was clearly one of them.

He walked back toward the kitchen area and then turned abruptly again and hurled the bottle of Jim Beam into the wall.

He'd wanted a nice dramatic smash of glass exploding against wall. But the bottle didn't break. The open mouth sprayed whiskey everywhere, sure, but then it slid quite undramatically to the floor.

And then he started to cry.

Just like that. No warning.

Standing there all macho with his .45 tucked in his belt and no shirt or shoes. And he started sobbing. Brought his hands to his head and clamped them tight, as if his head were going to fly apart in ugly pieces.

She went to him and I didn't blame her. Not the way he

sounded. All those years of grief—I doubted he'd cried much
in his life before this—overwhelming him now. He sounded
scared and tormented and angry and not a little bit pathetic.

I still didn't like him at all, but neither did I hate him quite
so much, either.

She held him. In that moment I imagine she was all the
women a man ever needed in his life—mother, sister, friend,
lover, protector.

She held him and he sobbed all the more. She finally led
him back to his chair.

I went over and picked up the Jim Beam bottle, which still
had some liquor in it. In the cupboard above the sink I found
a Kraft's jelly glass that felt sticky but looked reasonably
clean. I filled half of it with bourbon and carried it over to
him.

I figured we'd probably have one of those little moments.
You know, where the jerk comes to his senses and realizes
that it's a pretty all-right world after all.

But when I held the glass out to him all he did was yank
it out of my hand and say, "I want your white-boy ass out
of here, man."

Cindy looked up at me with lovely, tortured eyes. "He
doesn't mean it."

"Sure he does. He's a prick."

"Please . . ."

"I'll show you who's a prick, white boy."

He started up out of the chair at me and while I was not
exactly your macho type, the notion of putting my fist in his
face—even if he later pounded the hell out of me—sounded
pretty good, but Cindy stayed in her adult mode and got between us.

David sat back in the chair. Took some whiskey. He was
shaking so badly, his teeth chattered against the rim of the
glass. I had the sense that he might accidentally bite off a
chunk and cut himself. I'd seen it happen when people were
in psychotic states.

He decided to will me out of existence. From then on, he

didn't once look in my direction or acknowledge me in any way.

"You're the only one I can count on, babe."

Cindy had gone from bitch to babe in just a few short minutes. A promotion of sorts.

"I really need the money. You could have gotten it by now if you had really wanted to."

She shook her head. "Not until you tell me what's going on."

He went crazy again, pushing his face into hers, shouting with such force that he sprayed spittle everywhere. "Quit asking me questions!"

Then, abruptly, he froze, was quiet, listening.

He had good ears. Much better than mine.

Heard them coming and jumped to his feet. Ran back to his bedroom and grabbed his shirt and cowboy boots.

"David, what's wrong?" she said.

He held his hand up for silence.

We listened.

After a few seconds, I heard it. A heavy car rolling down the narrow street. Tires crunching gravel. Coming toward this trailer.

"David!"

She went to grab for him but he was too fast. He was out the screen door before she could even say his name again.

Nothing dramatic. No big goodbye speeches. He was just gone.

She went after him but I gently took her arm. "You'll never catch him."

"I have to help him." She was starting to cry.

"You can't help him. Not now."

Outside, the car pulled up to the trailer. The lights stayed on.

She glanced out the window. "It's my boss. Chief Gibbs."

"Yes," I said. "I kind of figured it would be."

ELEVEN

You might easily mistake Police Chief Richard Gibbs for a smalltown druggist or the crabbiest teacher in junior high. He had squinty eyes, stooped shoulders, thin lips that always looked just about to be displeased, and gnarly arthritic hands. In his khaki uniform, with his sleek bald head, he might have been a Scoutmaster searching for some aggravating troops.

Until he saw Cindy, that is. And then he changed. A light, a kind and wise light, shone in the brown eyes. And he slid his arm around her with genuine tenderness. "How you doin', hon?"

She tried a smile. "Been better, I suppose."

"All right if we go inside?" said one of the two uniformed men on the trailer's front steps.

"That's what we got the search warrant for, wasn't it?" Gibbs said.

"Well, uh, yeah, I guess so."

"Then go the hell in."

They went the hell in.

Lights came on in the dirty windows.

The small trailer rocked and tilted under the assault of their weight.

Gibbs glared at me. "Who is this guy?"

"A friend of mine."

He glared at me a little more. "Oh yeah, that federal guy. Personally, they always gave me a pain in the ass."

I laughed. "Gee, and I imagine they were just thrilled about working with you, too."

He smiled. "I was about the crankiest bastard they ever saw. Worked a couple of kidnappings with those stuck-up sonsofbitches and gave them hell every chance I got."

He put his hand out. "But that don't mean that every one of you is a stupid sonofabitch."

I shook his hand. "Right. Take me—I'm probably not a stupid sonofabitch now, am I?"

With a perfectly straight face, he said, "Too early to tell." He turned back to Cindy. "Your David did it this time."

"Maybe I don't want to know."

Fond as he obviously was of her, he wanted her to hear. "You remember all these years what I told you?"

"Please don't give me a speech, Gibby. Not now. Later on, all right. But not now."

We were silhouettes in the squad-car headlights that lit the leprous wounds of the trailer wall. The stars were faint now. A coyote cried out long and lonely from the limestone cliffs.

"I got a call."

"From who?"

"Don't know."

"They didn't leave a name?"

"Right. No name," Gibbs said.

"And they said what?"

"They said I should look inside his car trunk."

"For what?"

The other two cops came back out. "He's gone, Chief," one of them said. He had a blond crew cut and needed to lose thirty pounds. Everything about him was smalltown in a comfortable way.

"I would've told you that," she said.

"That's bullshit, Cindy, and you know it," said the cop who'd done the talking. "I tried to arrest him for public drunkenness that time, and you was all over me."

"You were hurting him."

"You seem to forget he kicked me in the nuts."

"That's enough!" Gibbs said. "All we're concerned about right now is tonight. Not the past."

But I was glad I'd heard the exchange between Cindy and the other cop. It made me understand better why the radio dispatcher had spoken about her with so much contempt. Cops run interference for family members all the time, but there are limits and I sensed that Cindy had pushed those limits pretty far.

"Let's go take a look at the trunk."

I didn't have any doubt what we'd find.

All the time they were trying various keys and pries to get the trunk-lid up, I knew exactly what we'd find. Pictured it perfectly.

"Gimme those," Gibbs said after a time.

He went through three more keys. The third one turned a quarter-inch or so to the right but it still didn't open the trunk.

"I wish you weren't here," Gibbs said to Cindy. "You'd really hear me swear."

"Be my guest."

Gibbs went back to working on the trunk. The two uniformed cops exchanged winks. The Chief wasn't any better at this than they were.

Gibbs said, "If this next one don't work, I'm gonna open the damn thing with a screwdriver."

Lights were coming on in windows around us. Police in the middle of the night guaranteed excitement. Infants cried; dogs barked; a frontier train rattled through the dark.

The lock clicked free.

"Gimme that flashlight," he said, holding his hand out so one of his men could fill it with a long silver light.

The trunk popped open.

We all gathered round.

Gibby played the light inside.

Her arm had been taken off pretty cleanly. That was the first thing I noticed.

The second thing I noticed was that the blue of the naked body matched the blue of the arm I'd seen earlier. Two, three days dead she was, at least long enough for postmortem lividity to set in, the body filling with gas and distending the areas of chest, stomach and thighs. The brown eyes bulged and the tongue looked like an eel trying to escape the swollen lips.

There was talk, but I didn't hear it, and running back to call for additional help, but I didn't pay any attention to that, either.

By now I was fixed on what had been done to her face, specifically her nose.

Whoever had done it had made the remains as crude and ugly as possible.

In Indian lore, as in the lore of Ancient Egypt, one cut the nose from a woman's face so that no man would ever again desire her. The mutilated woman often wandered into the woods and lived out her days alone. At least, these are the tales still told, though there is evidence that some of these women in fact took up new mates, and that others were simply accepted by the tribe the way a crippled person might be. Maybe it was only the most hideously defaced who had to flee to the forest to hide for ever.

If she'd lived, this woman, who I now saw was a Native American, would have presented her plastic surgeon with some difficult problems. The killer had taken so much of the nose, and removed it so brutally, that only a bloody hole remained, one that was difficult to look at.

"He couldn't have done something like this, he couldn't have."

Cindy was talking to herself, but I could hear her quite clearly. She stood next to me in front of the open trunk.

Then she took my arm. "He didn't do it, Robert. Really he didn't."

Behind us, Gibbs said, "Cindy, could you come over here a minute, please?"

She shook her head. "You hear his voice?"

"Uh-huh."

"He's already got David convicted."

"You have to admit, this doesn't look real good."

"You think he'd be stupid enough to drive her around in his trunk?"

"You're a law officer, Cindy. You know how crazy people can get after they kill somebody. Especially if they've been drinking or something."

This time, she didn't take my arm. She grabbed it. "God-damn it, Robert, didn't you hear me? He didn't kill her! He really didn't."

Then she went off to see the Chief. She was going to tell him the same thing.

Meanwhile, I spent some more time following down my ghoulish occupation. I borrowed the Chief's flashlight. There's a little trick about postmortem lividity. Sometimes it can tell you if a body has been moved around in a cramped space, such as a car trunk. This means that even if the body has been moved, the lividity will indicate the original position. Sometimes it's helpful to know such things.

I knelt down next to the trunk, holding my breath—the stink being pretty bad—and started training my light up and down the right side of her body.

On the whole, I would rather have been back home with my cats sleeping on the bed next to me and a bowl of Cream of Wheat waiting to be microwaved in the morning.

2

ONE

On this part of the frontier, the cabins had generally been built of logs that had been squared with a broadax and stripped of their bark. The pioneers built cabins close to creeks and streams for the sake of the water supply; and in an area of woods that looked rife with wild game and crab apples and plums and haws; and where there was an abundance of prairie hay which, along with corn cobs and animal droppings, could be used for fuel in the long and harsh winters.

The pioneers would not have recognized the manor house perched above me on the bluffs. It sat on better than two acres of oaks and dogwoods, a brick Georgian Colonial that bespoke not only wealth and privilege but also a certain disdain for anybody who drove up the steep, winding driveway. The house itself seemed to sense that all visitors would be unworthy. The landscaping, which used vast maples and elms as walls to keep out prying eyes, only enhanced the sense of unwelcome.

I was two steps from my rental Chevrolet when I heard a tennis ball being *thwocked* back and forth. I decided not to try the front door.

Instead, I followed a narrow stone walk around the massive east side of the house. Below me, in a small valley, lay a most impressive tennis court. Not only was it a double court, it was an *illuminated* double court. Only one of the courts was presently being used. Claire and Perry Heston were playing, both looking fit and eager in their tennis whites that glowed in the early afternoon sunlight.

I was still sleepy and it showed in the slowness of my walk. I'd finally gotten to sleep around 9:00 A.M., after telling Chief Gibbs about finding the arm. He seemed wary of the fact that not only had I been one of the dreaded Feds—a criminal profiler, no less—but that I now possessed a private investigator's license and worked freelance for both law enforcement and criminal-defense attorneys. He didn't seem mollified at all that I was writing a book of Iowa history, and that I was presently occupied on a long chapter about law enforcement. He just couldn't find much to like about me at all.

I'd had five restless hours of sleep—sometimes when I take a certain amount of troubles to bed, I have nightmares about my wife's death again—when I was awakened by Cindy at my motel-room door.

She was no longer depressed and vulnerable. She was angry. She said that there were certain white men in this town who now had a good excuse to track and kill an Indian, namely David. She said that David would be too afraid and stubborn to turn himself in so, if he ever crossed paths with those men, he would fight back and they would kill him.

She said I had to help. *Had to*. There was nobody else she could turn to. She said she'd work the settlement, asking questions of anybody who knew David well, trying to find out about his relationship to the woman in the trunk. By now, I'd told her not only about the arm but also about the fire-gutted mansion I'd followed David to. I said I had a vague feeling that maybe the Hestons, and their hulking friend Bryce Cook, might know something about the old Victorian house. She pleaded with me to go talk to them.

So here I stood watching the Hestons play tennis.

From what I could see, and from what little I knew about the game, they looked reasonably good. They certainly looked energetic.

When Perry Heston finally realized who was walking down the stone steps toward him—he'd been glancing at me on and off for the past half-minute—he did a very strange thing.

He stopped playing altogether.

His wife's volley went zooming past his shoulder but he paid it no attention whatsoever.

He just stood, hands on hips, watching me.

His face bore the same disdain for weary travelers that the front of his house did.

Before I'd even reached the courts, he said, "Just what the hell are you doing here, Mr. Payne?"

"I came to talk to you."

"Not to me, Mr. Payne. Because I don't *want* to talk to you. Everything I ever had to say to you, I said last night. And now I want you the hell off my property."

Claire looked both slightly afraid and embarrassed. "Honey, why don't you give Mr. Payne a chance—"

"I won't give Mr. Payne a chance to do diddly shit."

"Honey, please—"

"Go in the house, Claire."

She started to say something but before she could get the words out, he repeated: "Go in the house."

Like a reluctant child, she looked first at him, then at me and then she leaned down and picked up a lime-green tennis ball, tucked her racket under her arm, and left.

She was just as gorgeous in the daylight, a forty-ish woman who took fierce pride in her face and body. She was going to battle time to her last breath. Only the melancholy of her blue eyes said that there was more to her than another fading country club beauty.

"He's really not a bad guy," she said to me as she came out of the door of the fencing.

"I'm sure we'll be great pals."

She paused a moment, and said, in a voice her husband wouldn't be able to hear, "I'm sorry about the girl being murdered, Mr. Payne."

"I told you to go in the house," Perry Heston said from the court.

There were probably at least two or three people on the planet who would refuse to obey a direct order from Perry Heston, but his wife was definitely not one of them.

"I need to go now," she said.

And was gone.

He came through the door in the cage, carrying his racket by the handle the way you'd carry a weapon.

Last night, he'd wanted to do a little public relations—a community leader probably shouldn't be seen beating somebody up in a parking lot—but this morning all he planned to show me was his contempt for my kind in general and me in particular.

"You've got some balls, I'll give you that, driving up here this way."

"I just have a few questions."

"I don't give a damn what you have, Sport. I just want you off my land."

"I don't think that David Rhodes killed the woman they found in his trunk."

"Meaning what exactly?"

"Meaning I'd like to know why you were pounding on David last night."

He tried for a smile but it came out a sneer. "Do you know who I am?"

"I've got a pretty good idea."

"You know who my best friend is?"

"Probably not."

"The Mayor of this town, that's who my best friend is. Is this starting to make any sense to you, pal? I mean, I can be more explicit if you want me to." He jabbed at me with his racket. I didn't give him the satisfaction of backing up. "You're not jackshit to me or anybody else in this town. Maybe the ex-FBI agent bullshit plays out in the sticks, but not around here." He pointed his racket to my car. "Now you can get your ass off my property or I'm going to throw it off. Understand?"

He didn't look all that tough—business leaders get an inflated sense of their own power, both social and physical—but then I'm not that tough either.

"You know something about the murder, Heston."

"I do, eh?"

I nodded. "So I'll be back."

"Going to pull your big bad gun on me again, Sport?"

As I got back to my rental, I saw Claire Heston carrying an armload of books over to her silver Jaguar. I walked across and opened the door for her.

She nodded her thanks. "Library books. Even as a little girl I always had to pay fines for bringing them back late. But the funny thing is, even when I put them in the car like this I don't take them back right away. They ride around with me until I need to go to the library again."

She started to lean in, to drop the considerable stack on the rear seat, but a few of the books tumbled on to the drive. I picked them up. There were two Agatha Christies, one Joan Hess, *True Crimes*, volume two, one Nancy Pickard, and one Robert J. Randisi.

"You must like mysteries," I said.

"A lot." She smiled. "I guess I still like to be scared the way I got when I was a little girl. Not horror movies, I mean. Real stuff. It's a lot scarier."

"It sure is."

She put the books inside, closed the car door.

"He's really a pretty decent man."

This seemed to be a trend lately. Perfectly nice women defending indefensible mates.

"I'm sure he is."

"That didn't sound very sincere, Mr. Payne." The smile went. "He came up the hard way, as they say. His father had a very small construction business and lived on the west side. There wasn't even enough money for my husband to finish college. But he got together with Bryce Cook and they worked very hard. These days, their company is the biggest exporter in Cedar Rapids."

"Your background seems different, Mrs. Heston."

An empty polite laugh. " 'To the manor born' as they say. My great-great-grandfather came up from Virginia and built a small but very profitable railroad and then proceeded to help put Cedar Rapids on the map. This town was his pride and joy. And then it got away from him, I'm afraid."

I wanted to hear the rest of it but she stopped then.

And even if she'd wanted to tell me, her husband wouldn't have let her. He came up from the tennis courts, saw me and said, "I thought I told you to get the hell off my property. Now!"

"I see what you mean about him being a pretty decent guy," I said.

She allowed herself a small smile that he didn't catch, and I saw then the first hint of anger in her eyes as she turned to confront her husband.

"It's Saturday."

"I know it's Saturday, Gilhooley."

"The Cubs are playing."

"You should be happy I'm distracting you," I said.

"They're not doing that bad this year, Payne. They're not in last place."

"Yeah, they're in next to last place."

"Well, that's something to be thankful for, isn't it?"

"I suppose."

"My apartment's a pit."

"Boy, there's a shock. Gilhooley with a messy apartment."

"You sonofabitch!"

"Thank you," I said.

"I mean the first baseman. He just dropped the ball."

"I really would be doing you a favor, Gilhooley. Coming over, I mean. Distracting you from the Cubs' humiliating themselves as usual."

"Who do you want to know about anyway?"

"Perry Heston."

"That asshole. He got lucky. A west-sider who picked up all the chips, including the beautiful socialite daughter with the one bad habit."

"Which is?"

"Booze. Three or four extended trips to detox programs around the country. None of them seem to work for long."

"I take it you don't like Perry Heston much?"

"He's a jerk but at least he didn't earn his money the way everybody else around here did."

"How did they earn theirs?"

He laughed. "The old-fashioned way. They inherited it."

I'd known Gilhooley back in my Reserve Officers Training Corps days at the University of Iowa (you know, turning college boys into soldiers). In those days, ROTC was mandatory. Gilhooley had been the only Maoist that I knew of in our unit.

"You said you had another appointment?" he prompted.

"Yeah," I said.

"Why don't you get over here about four, then?"

"That'd be great. I appreciate it."

"Sure thing, kiddo. And I wouldn't object if you brought some good whiskey."

"Jack Daniel's black be all right?"

"Jack Daniel's black would be just about right, kiddo. Just about right."

I recognized the blonde woman several blocks away. She wore a yellow blouse and white shorts and blue Keds. She came out of one of the back doors of the three-building concrete-block complex that was Heston-Cook Computer, Inc. Being Saturday afternoon, only a few cars were in the lot.

Evelyn Cook led her two kids to a blue Saab sedan, got

them inside, strapped into safety belts, then turned around to find me waiting there.

"Hi," she said.

"Hi." I liked her easy, open face and manner. "I thought I might talk to your husband."

The open face closed some. "He won't want to talk about David Rhodes, Mr. Payne. He and Perry discussed it and that was their decision. They don't want to talk about David to anybody."

"What if it's the police?"

She shook her head. "This isn't going to help Claire, you know."

"Oh?"

"She—well, she's been drinking again. Not a lot, but that's how it always starts. Just a little bit at a time. And now this publicity—she's very protective of the family name." She smiled. "I guess that's why it's better to be a west-side girl like me. You don't have to worry about sullying the family crest." Then she stopped herself. "That sounds cruel and I don't mean it to. Claire's my best friend and I love her. It's just—she has this thing about the family tradition. Her great-great-grandfather was one of the most important men in this town and then he had to withdraw. He became a hermit and died at a relatively young age."

She was a contrast to her friend Claire. No stunning beauty but a kind of healthy suburban sexuality and a real intelligence in the deep blue eyes and the calm very female voice.

I followed her gaze. Her husband Bryce was hulking toward us. He wore a red golf shirt and dark slacks. He obviously spent time body-building.

I readied myself for another confrontation like the one I'd had with his partner Perry, but Bryce came bearing gifts. He put out a hand and I put out mine and this time he didn't try to tear it from my shoulder and crush it.

"I'm glad I got a chance to see you again," he said. "I was into the sauce pretty good last night and being a real jerk. I'm sorry."

"I appreciate the apology, Cook."

"No problem." He glanced at his gold Rolex. "We're due at the Club in an hour. A *luau* tonight."

Evelyn smiled. "Bryce wants me to wear a hula skirt."

She would have looked damned fine in a hula skirt. Bryce knew what he was talking about.

"I know why you're here," Bryce Cook said. "It's about David Rhodes, isn't it? We had some trouble, is all. Nothing whatsoever to do with that woman they found dead or anything. Gambling stuff, actually."

"Gambling?"

He nodded. "There are a few after-hours places in Cedar Rapids and that's where we met Rhodes. He accused us of cheating him and that's why he started coming after us, making trouble. You know what I mean."

"Gambling," I said. It was a nice, slick story and I didn't believe a word of it.

"Gambling." Then, "You go get in the car, hon."

She nodded. "Nice to see you again, Mr. Payne."

"Nice to see you."

She went around and got in the car and shut the door.

Bryce Cook moved a little closer to me and spoke in a low voice. It was meant to assure me, this gesture of intimate good friendship, that now he was going to tell me the *real* truth.

"Actually, it was about this woman. This after-hours place I mentioned?"

"Right."

"Well, there was this woman there and Perry and I were kind of drunk and we were hustling her a little bit and—well, you know how it goes."

"And David Rhodes—"

"Rhodes gets bent all out of shape and starts hassling us. And keeps hassling us. So finally, the other night we go to the casino—not even knowing he worked there—and he starts hassling us again, this time in front of our wives. That's why we took him outside on our break and punched him around a little. He was getting to be a real pain in the ass over this really minor deal. You know?"

Another very slick story that didn't quite seem real.

But how could I argue with it?

"You can see the kind of guy we're dealing with, right?" he said. "The way he cut that Indian woman up? God."

One more glance at his Rolex for my sake. "Hey, I've really got to go. Take care of yourself, right?"

Evelyn waved at me as they drove away in their nice new snug Saab.

I waved back with a genuine sense of loneliness. I really did sort of like her.

TWO

After stopping off at City Hall to check on deeds and prop-
erties, I spent the early afternoon in the downtown branch of
the Cedar Rapids Library going through books about the city
at the turn of the century.

It's always fun to imagine that there was a kinder, gentler
time even if that sort of nostalgia is largely a fantasy. The
photographs deceive. How simple and amiable life looks in
the faded snapshots of women in big fancy bustles and men
in sideburns and bowlers. Barbershop quartets serenading lov-
ers as they stroll along the moonlit Cedar River; horseless
carriages bedazzling the children who chase after them down
the street; and trolley cars pulled by a mule.

Kinder, gentler.

Until you look more closely at the faces in the faded photographs and see in their eyes all the griefs, all the fears, all the heartache we know today.

The human condition has probably been the same since that first ancient ancestor of ours, in whatever form he took, struggled from the ocean to collapse on the beach, starving for food, shelter and some sense of why he'd been put on this planet in the first place.

It is this reality that the old photos rarely convey, except in the pictures of the Civil War with the broken and dead strewn across the bloody ground, or the Nevada executions where three men were hanged at once, or in the crazed and aggrieved eyes of the darky slaves as they slink from the plantation house to the filth and grime of their own abodes.

You have to be careful with the happy old photos. They can trick you into believing that at one time there was this human race completely different from our own.

> *Tobacco is a filthy weed that*
> *From the Devil does proceed.*
> *It drains your purse, it*
> *Burns your clothes. And makes*
> *A chimney of your nose.*

(Admonition to schoolchildren, 1886)

I always go through a few old history books every time I'm in a library. I usually turn up something for my notebooks. I don't know that I'll ever use all the notes I have but they're pleasant to compile.

But my real task was finding a book on the homes of the Cedar Rapids élite. It took a while but I found one.

The burned-out Victorian house I'd been in the other night did not appear in the book.

I looked through three different histories of the city. Many, many wealthy homes were alluded to and shown. But not the one I wanted.

I asked a woman at the reference desk if there were any

more books on local architecture. She said there were, and told me where I'd find them.

It was a lazy afternoon, and it felt good and comfortable and fun to be inside the library, the way it had always felt when I was a young boy searching the shelves for science fiction and mysteries.

I spent an hour there but found out exactly nothing about the mystery house.

Then I started looking up the history of the Ashlock family in Cedar Rapids. The kin of Claire Heston *née* Ashlock had done well by themselves and the city. Local Ashlocks could be found in business, medicine, government, the arts (though I wasn't sure what that meant) and law. Great-great-grandfather's first name had been Douglas and a fine-looking, generous man he'd been, helping hospitals, symphony orchestras, soup kitchens, prisons and churches with his millions. And then, in 1903, something seemed to have happened. Several stories in the main newspaper suggested trouble without saying anything specific. It was duly noted that, over a period of four months, Douglas Ashlock a) resigned as President of his railroad b) resigned from his position on the Mayor's Select Committee c) resigned from the board of Trawler College (the local liberal arts school) d) took an extended trip to Europe—which proved to be longer than a year. After that, there was very little mention of the once-prominent man. Not until his funeral six years later was he depicted on the front page again.

Something terrible had happened to Douglas Ashlock—but what?

———◆———

Frontier historians generally complain about how money could always buy off justice on the plains. But this was no less true in any other part of the country. Of course, justice was for sale in Kansas and Texas and Oklahoma—just as it was for sale in New York and New Hampshire—and London and Paris.
                    Professor David Cromwell's Indian Journal

Deep summer came, a time of picnics and roller-skating and boating and minstrels and, Anna's favorite, chautauquas, at one of which she heard a stirring young woman proclaim: "Away, and for ever, with the idea that a married woman can make no progress in study. It is difficult sometimes to make women believe this and to dispossess them of the idea that marriage is an insuperable barrier to education."

And then there was the murder trial.

Even with all the windows open in the courtroom, the temperatures scaled ninety degrees and over. Fans could be heard flapping, loud as bird wings.

There were only a few seats for spectators and these were allotted each morning by drawing straws.

Indians appeared in small groups every so often and stood in the back of the courtroom.

Tall Tree sat glumly, watching the lawyers perform their lawyerly tasks, rarely saying anything except once when a witness described the dead woman as "beautiful and delicate of soul."

The curious thing was, nobody seemed to know where the young woman had come from—or where she lived.

The presumption was that she'd been raised on one of the nearby settlements. Yet nobody stepped forth to claim her.

The other presumption—since she was so often seen shopping in Cedar Rapids—was that she was from town. But, again, nobody stepped forward to claim her.

Anna attended court one day. She spent most of the time watching Tall Tree. In a way she could not explain, she believed devoutly in his innocence.

All the time she was in court, she played with the strange black moon fishing lure that Douglas Ashlock had given his friends. By now, she had evolved her own theory of the crime. Douglas Ashlock, for a reason Anna did not yet know, had killed the young woman.

As for Trace Wydmore, he and Anna had broken up somewhere in the vicinity of 220 times.

She would let him get to second base and then start to feel like a harlot again and then break up with him again and then miss him so much that she'd give in to him when he came around again (first base only) and then spend half the night sitting up in the kitchen talking to Mrs. Goldman.

"The terrible thing is, I enjoy it, Mrs. Goldman."

"That's only natural, Anna. To enjoy sex."

"For a woman to enjoy sex?"

Mrs. Goldman smiled. "Yes, of course. My late husband and I were quite compatible."

"You did?"

"Sure. Sex is a part of life, Anna."

"But Trace and I aren't married yet."

"Then maybe you should get married."

"That's the problem."

"What is?"

"I love him but I don't know if I love him enough to marry him. I mean, I read those women's magazines and they talk about the real thing and when I compare what they say to how I feel about Trace, then I'm not sure it's the real thing."

Mrs. Goldman yawned and then stretched her hand across the kitchen table and patted Anna's hand with great maternal affection. "Maybe I have the solution, Anna."

"Oh?" Anna said anxiously. "What is it?"

"Stop reading those magazines."

THREE

According to Ressler, Burgess and Douglas—among the most knowledgeable criminologists in the world—a homicide that involves mutilation serves several purposes for the murderer.

1. He is able to make ugly something he fears and loathes i.e. a face, breasts, sexual organs etc.

2. It is the mutilation after death, not the act of killing, that frequently brings him sexual satisfaction.

3. This type of satisfaction is onanistic i.e. masturbatory. Only rarely are sexual fluids

discovered in the cavities of the victim. Far more
often, fluids are found on or around the body. For
the killer, the ultimate fantasy—the sexual thrill
of mutilation—occurs after death.

4. There is also the phenomenon of regressive
necrophilia, when the killer places foreign objects
inside the victim.

I went through twenty pages of material in the book while I
waited for Claire Heston to descend the steep driveway from
her manor house and drive into town. I planned to follow her
and talk to her, if I could. I wanted to know more about her
great-great-grandfather, Douglas Ashlock.

I still had an hour and a half to go before I saw Gilhooley.
The overcast afternoon was humid. I ran the air condition-
ing until my sinuses started to protest.

The Hestons lived on a stretch of road that ultimately became Marion, a small town adjacent to Cedar Rapids. This
was the preferred area for the new rich. Even if I hadn't
known that, the parade of expensive foreign cars would have
given me a clue.

I returned to my reading, this time learning about a fellow
who had sex with his victims both before and after their
deaths. Once he'd even managed to have sex while the victim
was dying. The clever fellow used a garrote.

These were characteristics of the sexual mutilator. I was
trying to apply them to what I knew about the two women
who had been killed. This kind of sifting would be made
easier with a computer.

I also needed to see the autopsy on the woman who'd been
found in David Rhodes' trunk. With that information, I could
tap into my home computer and do some background work.

At first I didn't recognize the driver of the red BMW. It
came fast down the curving drive, paused only briefly, and
then turned right on to the street.

He was headed west. My good friend Perry Heston.

I decided, just for the hell of it, just, I suppose, because I was tired of waiting for Claire, to follow him.

In broadstroke, Cedar Rapids used to divide neatly into two parts, the river splitting the town in half.

On the east side, the further away from the river you got, you had the middle classes and the upper middle classes and then the very wealthy. The west side was largely working class, though even that was subdivided by several factors— race, steady employment (a good factory job was worth more than menial labor) and aspirations. Men who wore neckties to work (even if they sold shoes) did not want to live in the same kind of house a truck driver did.

This all started to change in the eighties when the yuppies decided to democratize Cedar Rapids i.e. start building on the west side where land prices were cheaper. Today the east side still has the greatest number of upper-class and wealthy people, but the west side also has its share of climbers, boomers and yuppies, everybody from cut-rate dentists to advertising executives. And, because the gods of urban planning seem to like such ironies, the west side can no longer claim the roughest parts of the city. No, they're now to be found on the east side, all the Chicago drug-gang members who moved out here to tap a new market (not unlike Amway with guns)— drugs and numbing poverty and terrifying violence all now within less than a few miles of where some of the better folks live. I recently saw a little black girl run into the middle of the street. She was as ragged and filthy and frightened-looking as a waif you might see on a TV show about famine. You never used to see this in Cedar Rapids. And you didn't have one or two shootings a night, either. Drugs have turned all small cities into bad imitations of the bigger ones.

My pal Perry took me over to the west side.

I used to live out there back when there was still some pastureland and fast silver creeks and ragged piney hills. I had a horse named Buck and a dog named Timmy and a sister named Jane and we all played together and had a great grand time, especially in the fall when the leaves were turning and the air was intoxicating with a smoky scent.

You couldn't imagine any of that now. Maybe as many as 1,000 housing units packed both sides of the street. This was the new working class, better fed, clothed, housed and educated than the old one, and yet paying at least a small price for it by being packed together this way.

We drove twenty blocks and then turned right, toward the bluffs and apartment houses and condo units that the yuppies had brought along with them.

He crossed the long bridge that spans the Cedar River and then turned left, up into the highest of the piney hills. He came to a gate marked PRIVATE and stopped. He took a garage-door opener from his glove compartment and opened the gate. He drove through.

I watched all this through my trusty Swarovski field glasses, the ones the Bureau let me take along when I resigned. I sat across the road, staring.

Through the pines at the top of the hill, I could see the shape of a Chalet-style house. Perry pulled in there, got out of his car and went up to the front door. He walked very fast. He was smoking a cigarette with hard fast anxious drags.

The rest I couldn't see.

The next ten minutes, I did some more reading about sexual mutilation—not a subject you want to embrace right before dinner-time—and kept an idle eye on the house where Perry Heston had gone. I had the sense that he was on some urgent kind of mission. I often have this sense of things. And most of the time I'm wrong.

This time, however, I was right.

They came out of the house, the two of them, moving fast.

There was a very pretty young woman with him. She wore a red blouse, tight black slacks. Her outsize dark glasses, vivid red lips and perfect cheekbones gave her the look of a starlet.

Perry Heston carried a large buff blue suitcase.

He put the young woman in the shotgun seat, stuffed the suitcase in the back seat, and then got in the car and started up the engine.

He backed down the driveway very fast.

By now I was pretty sure that something was very wrong indeed.

I felt an excitement that was probably uncharitable. The grief of others shouldn't give me a thrill.

But I just kept thinking of him slamming his fist into David Rhodes' stomach. And then it was real hard to feel sorry for him. Real hard.

He disappeared behind the pines for a time.

I almost suspected that he might have turned around and gone back to the house.

But then suddenly he was in my field glasses.

He came down the hill fast and turned east.

Framed in the circles of my field glasses, he looked quite unhappy. He was smoking hard and fast again and waving a hand that frequently became a fist.

The young woman still looked quite beautiful. But now, fixed in my glasses the way she was, I noticed something else about her.

She was an Indian.

FOUR

We drove twenty more minutes, ending up at a recently constructed apartment house out on First Avenue. I parked and watched as he pulled the BMW around the back and then toted the blue suitcase inside. She followed.

I was already late for my meeting with Gilhooley but I decided to give it a few more minutes here. I reversed down the street where I could get a good view of the back of the place.

The tan building went ten stories and was too fancy for my taste. There was a lot of glass and a lot of timber and nice landscaping, but it took a little too much pride in itself to be suitable for human occupation.

Six of the verandas were occupied and all of the occupants

were elderly. White hair and knobbly knees shone in the fading sunlight. Just the sort of retirement I'd always envisioned for my late wife and myself, actually. Two elderly people still very much in love, sipping their lemonades on a breeze-blessed veranda, watching the sun sink behind the pines and hearing the sweet songs of the nightbirds only Iowa can claim.

Perry Heston brought the Indian girl out on her veranda a few minutes later. They both carried drinks. Their heads bobbed and pointed at each other. They were arguing.

He said something and she spat at him.

He stood unmoving, stunned.

Then he threw his drink in her face and disappeared back inside the apartment.

She walked over to the veranda door and stuck her head inside. I imagined she was yelling something at him.

Seventh floor, middle.

I had to remember that for when I tried to sneak in here tonight.

Now it was time for Gilhooley.

"You know how big a shit our government is, Payne?"

"You don't need to tell me, Gilhooley."

"All it cares about is taking care of the fat cats."

Two things you have to know about Gilhooley. He's a Maoist. Or says he is. And he measures all politics against Mao's politics. The second thing is, he's made a real study of Cedar Rapids and what he doesn't know, he can find out. He can be a valuable source of information.

He smiled. "This is good booze. I appreciate it. Plus it's great to argue with somebody bright. Most people just walk away when I start talking politics."

Gee, really, Gilhooley, I wonder why? Couldn't be because you're a fanatic or anything, could it?

I go back a number of years with the guy. When we were at the University of Iowa together, we used to go drinking every night just so we could argue. I was always a conservative and he was always a radical—not liberal, *radical*. He numbered, among the people he admired, George McGovern, Jane Fonda and Jerry Brown. I admired, among others, Barry Goldwater, Dwight Eisenhower and Joan Didion (a lot more conservative a thinker than many people realize).

The battle continued on, even after I joined the Bureau, even after Gilhooley became associate editor of a left-wing magazine published out of Cedar Rapids.

Any time I thought he might have changed, all I had to do was look around his tiny, dusty, littered apartment.

JESUS SAVES
(Green Stamps)

was the sign he had tacked to his door, the same one he'd used way back in college, when Green Stamps were still being made.

Gilhooley had been married three times but not a trace of domesticity had ever rubbed off on him. His idea of a formal occasion was one for which he had to tuck in his sports shirt. He took out his garbage at least twice a month, three times if Christmas was coming up, and he picked up the debris in his living room—Domino pizza boxes, beer cans, girly magazines, dirty clothes—only when he needed to find a place for a guest to sit down. The guest was usually a woman. You might not think of a gangly red-haired Maoist Irishman as an ass-bandit—but somehow he was.

But even more than the clutter, his wobbly bookcase defined Gilhooley's soul. To him, it would always be 1970, with a whiff of tear gas on the air, an ROTC building in flames in the background, and a Jefferson Airplane song on everyone's lips.

In his bookcase you found battered paperbacks by Eldridge Cleaver, Timothy Leary, Bernadette Dorn, Danny the Red, Eugene McCarthy and Bobby Seale among many, many others.

Indeed, for Michael Patrick Gilhooley, it would always be 1970.

He ran a hand through curly strawberry-blond hair that was

slowly showing gray and said reflectively, "Perry Heston and Bryce Cook, huh? You could get in a *lot* of trouble . . ." He grinned. I suppose it gave him pleasure watching a Republican like me cast in the role of working-class hero.

"They look like players."

"Oh they are, they are—you know that kind of corporate macho bullshit you see so much today. They've got fortunes, they've got beautiful wives, they've got beautiful mistresses, and they relax by doing a little bullfighting on the side."

I laughed. "I didn't know there was a whole lot of bull-fighting in Iowa."

"You know what I mean. All the macho shit these guys get into."

"Perry Heston didn't come from a rich family, right?"

"Oh, no. Horatio Alger all the way. In fact, at the time he married Claire Ashlock, people said that he was going to take that old respectable family and give it some new life and that's just what he did. Sort of like introducing some pit-bull blood into a line of Pekinese. Not that he'll ever be quite acceptable to the real upper crust—you know, westside boy trying to pass himself off as the Real Thing and all that bullshit. And he does get in some trouble. I mean, he looks like the ultimate corporate player but he really is a chaser—booze and ladies and even a few fights from time to time. He's brought the Ashlock family back to prominence again, but at a certain cost to their old reputation. He had the money and she had the name."

"She didn't have any money at all?"

"Not so's you'd notice. You know the Balzac line, 'Behind every fortune there's a scandal'?"

"Sure."

"Well, the Ashlocks had had a lot of money until something happened to Great-great-grandpapa."

"That was going to be my next question. What happened?"

"Some kind of scandal. It broke the great-great-grandfather of the family, the one who made all the money. He ended up in an insane asylum. I mean, the Ashlocks—including

Claire's parents—always had enough money to keep up appearances, but that was about it.''

''What kind of scandal with Great-great-grandpapa?''

''Not sure. But I can find out from a friend of mine, this old Labor guy who used to publish the Labor paper here.''

''There was a Labor paper in Cedar Rapids?''

''Sure, back around the turn of the century, then intermittently up until the fifties.''

One hundred years ago, Cedar Rapids, like other midwestern communities of its size, could claim as many as ten daily and weekly newspapers, between them covering the whole spectrum of political beliefs and social concerns. I hadn't known that any of them lasted until the fifties.

''Anyway, Sullivan, he's in his late eighties now and knew all the old newspaper people in this town. I'm sure he can tell me what happened to Ashlock.''

''You never heard any scuttlebutt, then?''

Gilhooley shrugged. ''Some, I guess. One was that his wife caught him in bed with one of the domestics and later killed the girl and that the old man had to bury her and cover everything up. And that he was so ashamed of what all his carousing had done to his wife that he just gradually withdrew from everything.''

''Anything else?''

''Well, there was one that the old man accidentally killed his mistress and had to cover that up.'' He looked at me and smiled. ''You're really getting into this, aren't you, Robert?''

''I want to know who I'm dealing with.''

''All that great FBI training you had.'' He arched an eyebrow. ''Did you ever stop to think that the FBI and the Jesuits are a lot alike?''

''I think you've told me that before,'' I said patiently. ''About six hundred times, if I'm not mistaken.''

Of all the Machiavellian organizations in the world, according to Gilhooley anyway, the two worst are the FBI and the Jesuits.

''Any other rumors?'' I said.

''The Circle of Six,'' he announced.

"The what?"

"Some kind of secret society. This was back near the turn of the century, remember. Victoriana was a big part of life for the gentry out here. You saw a fair share of hansom cabs parked outside Greene's Opera House downtown, and a lot of people affected Edwardian-style clothes. And had secret societies. You know what I mean, you're a big Sherlock Holmes fan."

"And Ashlock was part of this secret society?"

"That was the rumor. But first of all, Payne, you've got to understand that there was this whole group of rich Anglophiles living in Cedar Rapids then. They went to Britain every few years and brought back everything British they could, including this English thing for secret societies. Hell, in those days, you still had vestiges of the Thugs." He grinned. "Not to mention the Masons."

"Who were the Thugs?"

His grin widened. "Very bad folks is what those were. The Assassins originated in Egypt back around A.D. 1000, and one of the things they were noted for was killing anybody their leaders told them to. The killer usually dressed in a white tunic with a red sash and he was absolutely fearless. He usually used a dagger. Every king in Europe was afraid of these people. They were absolute fanatics—and very successful, despite the white tunics and red sashes. Apparently they murdered seven European leaders in three centuries.

"One of their favorite routines was to kidnap somebody they hated, fasten him to a cross with rope—and then ask a young man who wanted to be a Thug to set him on fire. If the young man could do it, he was automatically made a Thug."

"You think Ashlock was into some kind of violence?"

He shrugged again. "I don't know, but I doubt it. In Victorian England, there were a lot of secret societies involving sexual activities of various kinds. I suspect that's probably what the good burghers of Cedar Rapids were up to. But you're a good ex-FBI man, Payne; you should be able to figure it out."

"A secret that's over a hundred years old?"

He grinned again. "You're the detective, my friend."

"So after this thing happened—whatever it was—the Ashlocks lost all their money?"

"Not all of it. As I said, the old man went into the asylum and died there, and a grandson looked after the estate. They always had money—I think Claire Heston probably still has some of her own today—but not big money. Not power money. And in a town like Cedar Rapids, nobody pays any attention to you unless you have power money." He laughed out loud. "But you're still working on The Circle of Six, aren't you? I knew that'd get you. Who could resist a secret society?"

Actually I wasn't thinking about a secret society at all. I was thinking about how I was going to get into the apartment house where Perry Heston had installed the beautiful young Indian woman.

"So you'll let me know when you talk to this old reporter friend of yours?"

"Sullivan? Sure. But he's back east visiting his daughter so it may be a while."

The phone rang. He grabbed it and said, "Hey, hi."

The way he said it, I knew it was a woman. Nothing focused Gilhooley's mind like the opposite sex. And I could tell that he suddenly wished I wasn't there.

I obliged him. We went through one of those brief pantomimes wherein I gestured that I needed to be going and he gestured back (insincerely) that I should stay, and then I was at the door and out.

Mother night was drawing the drapes, and the air was chill, and the stars were many and bright, and I thought of my wife, as I did at so many odd moments, and felt a terrible loneliness.

———◄•►———

It is when we examine the death penalty that we see how skewed justice was for people of red or black skin. Time and again red men would be hanged while white

men served life sentences (some with the possibility of parole) for the same offense.
                              Professor David Cromwell's Indian Journal

Mid-August—and a blazing mid-August it was, with ice wagons clopping up and down the street night and day—Tall Tree was found guilty by the jury and told by the Judge that he would be hanged at the state penitentiary early next year.

The sentence pushed Anna into further action.

She began carrying around with her the scrap of paper she had found at the crime scene:

> *ay*
> *ouse*

Whenever she got a chance, she showed the paper to people and asked them if they could guess what it would read if the other half hadn't been torn away.

People made some pretty intriguing guesses:

F(*ay*) Cl(*ouse*)—a citizen
M(*ay*) H(*ouse*)—a café
B(*ay*) S(*ouse*)—nickname for cheap whiskey-
   drinker

And so on.

And then one day Anna had to run an errand for the Chief and she stopped to see a courthouse friend who worked in deeds and titles, a spiffy man with a handlebar mustache and a hankering to take Anna over to Tilden's drugstore and sit there during the lunch-hour wooing her with fountain Coca-Colas.

Anna hadn't tried the torn note on him before so she thought she'd give it a try and her friend took a look at it and said immediately: "Gray House."

"Gray House? What's that?"

"This mansion that Douglas Ashlock built for himself—

and then his wife decided it was too far away from town so they built another big house here.''

"Does he still use it?"

Tilden smiled. "He and his friends do, from what I hear. That's where they go when they want to do serious drinking and carousing."

"Must be nice to have a spare mansion."

"Yeah, it must be, mustn't it?"

That very same night, Anna started spending most of her evenings following Douglas Ashlock around. She knew how dangerous this was—a word from Ashlock to the Mayor and Anna would be fired—but she had no choice. An innocent man sat waiting to be hanged.

"May I ask you a question, Mrs. Goldman?"

"Why, sure, Anna."

"Were you a virgin when you got married?"

"That's quite a question."

"I'm sorry if I embarrassed you."

"That's all right, you didn't embarrass me. And the answer is, yes, I was."

"May I ask you one more question?"

"I think that'd probably be all right." They were standing in the kitchen and Mrs. Goldman gave Anna a little hug. "Honey, I know what you're going through with Trace so ask me as many questions as you want."

"Did you ever let him get to second base before you were married?"

"Second base?"

Anna explained.

Mrs. Goldman laughed. "That's a good one. But no, the answer is that he didn't get any further than first base."

"So you don't think I'm being crazy?"

"Honey, you need to do what feels right to you. If you don't want to let him get to second or third base, then just tell him that."

"I'm going to lose him."

"I don't think so."

"Have you ever seen Marietta down at the soda fountain?"

"She's pretty, I'll say that for her."

"She's prettier than I am, that's for sure."

"But she doesn't have your intelligence or your fire, Anna."

"She doesn't?"

"Not at all."

"Thanks for saying that, Mrs. Goldman. I appreciate it."

"Second base and third base and home run," Mrs. Goldman laughed as she left the kitchen. "I just can't believe this modern age."

FIVE

My next stop was at Linda Prine's, me scooting in right behind a car that had a buzzer for the gate. The driver didn't even look at me. Probably worn out from a long day at the office. With dusk making everything hushed and melancholy, he probably just wanted to get up to his condo and relax.

I followed the guy up to the right rear door. Only now did he look inquisitive. He was in his early sixties, wearing a blue seersucker suit, a white button-down shirt, blue regimental striped tie and black horn-rimmed glasses that all said "lawyer." His leather briefcase only confirmed my suspicions.

"I'm sorry," he said. "I guess I don't know you."

"I'm Perry's cousin from Des Moines."

"Well, I'll be damned. His cousin."

I nodded.

"Well, hell, glad to meet you."

He was wiry and silver-haired but his grip had lost none of its power.

"Perry is one of our favorite people—my wife and I, I mean."

"He's a great guy."

He smiled. "You forgot your key, right?"

"Right."

"You ask that cousin of yours how many times I've had to let him in. He keeps his place just down the hall from us." He winked. "You know, for his extra-curricular activities."

All the way in, all the way up the elevator he talked about how the Hawks looked for the coming football season.

"Great as usual," I said.

"That's what I think."

After we got off on the proper floor, he turned to the left. I'd managed to notice in the lobby that Perry's number was 1012. Which meant I went right.

"Thanks again for everything," I said.

"If you're not busy later, stop down and we'll have a drink on the veranda."

"That sounds nice. Appreciate it."

Then he was gone.

"Who is it?"

"Perry."

"Perry? What happened?"

"Can't find my key."

"Oh, shit."

She might be gorgeous, the young Indian woman in Perry's apartment, but she wasn't real friendly.

Nor was she particularly careful.

She opened the door and there I stood and I wasn't Perry at all.

"You're not Perry."

"I guess I'm not."

"How would you like it if I screamed?"

"I'm not sure Perry would appreciate it if you attracted attention in a high-tone place like this."

"You asshole."

"Thanks, I'll take that as an invitation to come in and have a drink."

I went in and closed the door behind me. She didn't offer me a drink.

"You're one of those bastards from the County Attorney's office, aren't you? They want me to talk about David."

County Attorney. I wondered what she was talking about.

The condo was a showplace of taste and money—a living room of three club chairs and two small couches done in cream-colored leather, a fireplace that gave the room its focus, and two full walls of built-in bookcases.

Behind me, as I walked around gawking, she said, "Why don't you just give it to me and leave?"

I turned to look at her. She wore a white bikini top and tight white jeans. Her middle was bare and it was brown and cried out to be nibbled on. Her shining dark eyes and shining dark hair gave her a sexual presence that was somehow oppressive.

"Give you what?"

"The subpoena."

"What subpoena?"

She sighed, set nice little hands on nice little hips. "Look, Perry is going to be back and he's been drinking and if he sees you here, there'll be a scene. So just give it to me and get the hell out of here."

"I'm not from the County Attorney's office."

"Then where are you from?"

"I'm helping Cindy Rhodes."

Her beautiful face was soured by a frown. "Good old Cindy."

"You don't like her?"

She laughed harshly. "Why, I thought everybody liked Cindy."

"What's wrong with her?"

"Other than being a sanctimonious bitch who's ashamed of the fact that she's Native American, nothing."

"She doesn't think that David killed the woman they found in his car trunk."

Her eyes averted from mine. "I wouldn't know."

"The dead woman's name was Karen Moore. Did you know her?"

"No." But she said it too quickly. And she still couldn't quite look me in the eye.

"What's your name?" I asked.

"Linda Prine. And I shouldn't even tell you that."

I walked over to the veranda. Looked out. Cedar Rapids, with its ring of rolling bluffs, really was a lovely city.

"I imagine it's nice just sitting up here at night."

"I don't have time for this bullshit, man. If you're through, why don't you leave?" But she came out on the veranda with me and took deep breaths of the smoky autumn-like night.

"How many men share this apartment?"

"That isn't any of your business."

"Bryce and Perry Heston is all?"

"You heard what I said, man. None of your business."

"What happens when you start getting a few lines on your face and your breasts start to sag a little?"

"Ever hear of plastic surgery?"

"Yeah, but there's one thing about men like Cook and Heston. 'They wanted fresh new meat to carve.' That's a line from an old blues song."

"I'm the fresh new meat?"

"You are for now. But pretty soon it'll be somebody else."

"I can see why you and Cindy get along so good, man. You like being sanctimonious, too."

I leaned on the edge of the veranda and looked out at the rolling acres and thought of how hard it had been for the pioneers to settle this land. I'd recently read a journal kept by a Rhode Island woman who came halfway here in a covered wagon. The other half she'd had to walk. She arrived alone even though she'd started out with a husband and four children. She'd lost them, variously, to drowning, cholera (her twins) and a prairie fire that she described as "burning every-thing that I could see with these sad old eyes of mine." The journal stopped right after she reached Ioway Territory as it was then called, and I often wondered about her, how she'd ended up, her sweetness and dignity and sorrow.

The front door burst inward.

I didn't have to speculate who it might be.

By the time I had a chance to turn around, Perry Heston stalked into the living room.

I had the feeling he wasn't going to offer me a drink, either.

"What the hell are you doing here?"

He tried to look cool and casual in his pink polo shirt and chinos but he was too sweaty and agitated to make that kind of impression.

She was angry. "What do you think, I'd tell him something he could use against us?"

"I want him out of here."

"I want him out, too. But there's no need to get rough."

He turned back to me. "If I ever see you around here again, Jerk Off, you're going to be very, very sorry."

"I want to know about Karen Moore. You don't usually hang out with women in their forties. What made her so special?"

He glared over his shoulder at the woman.

She shook her head, apparently meaning that she'd told me nothing.

"I don't know any Karen Moore," he said to me.

"Right."

"I don't give a shit if you believe me or not, Sport. In fact, I don't give a shit about anything except you walking out that door right now."

He made a grab for me but I stepped back. I wasn't afraid of him and I think he sensed this and it seemed to calm him down a little.

"Whatever it is, Heston, I have a feeling it's all going to come out real soon." I smiled at him. "Just the way The Circle of Six came tumbling down."

The woman looked afraid, as if she agreed with me.

"I want you out. Now."

He wasn't yelling anymore. In fact, he looked tired, and much older, suddenly. The gray hair didn't look so premature.

"You hear me?"

"I hear you."

"Then, out."

I nodded to Linda Prine. "I'd still like to talk to you sometime."

I left. Before I even quite got the door closed, Heston was shouting at her.

SIX

There were two Patricia Moores listed in the Cedar Rapids phone book. I tried the one with the worst address.

A woman, who did not necessarily sound sober, said, "Hello."

"I'm calling about Sandy Moore."

There was a pause. "Who is this, anyway?"

"My name is Robert Payne."

"Well, Robert Payne, Sandy Moore is dead."

"I know that. I want to talk to somebody about her."

"Why?"

"I'm doing some work for a client of mine. I'm a private investigator."

"They got the guy who killed her. That bastard Rhodes."

"You knew Sandy?"

"Knew her? Is this a joke or something?"

"Ma'am, I just need to talk to somebody who knew her. About her background."

"I'm her daughter."

"I'm sorry for all this trouble but could I stop over and see you?"

"This place is a pit."

I thought of Gilhooley. Nothing could be more of a pit than his place.

"I'm sure it'll be fine."

"Don't try and tell me that bastard didn't kill her."

"Why don't we talk when I get there?"

"He killed her. He killed her for sure."

As a boy, I always used to go for Sunday drives with my mother and father. This was usually one of the neighborhoods we passed through when we drove around Cedar Rapids. But as the middle classes pushed further out Mount Vernon Road, the drug-pushers and muggers moved in to prey on the poor who now filled the houses and apartments.

I locked my car up nice and tight and tapped my shoulder-holster to make sure it was in its proper place.

The address was a crumbling stucco two-story. According to the mailbox, she lived on the second floor.

I climbed the stairs up through a haze of marijuana smoke, greasy cooking smells and the rot at the center of this old house.

She was playing something country and western when I knocked and she didn't bother to turn it down when she came to open the door.

She was short and dumpy in a loose, dirty housecoat. A cigarette burned in the same hand that held a can of generic supermarket beer. You could see she'd been pretty once, just like the house she lived in.

"You Payne?"

"Right."

"Tole you this was a pit."

"It's fine."

She laughed with great harsh self-loathing. "Yeah, a real fucking palace, isn't it?"

I walked in and sat down in a bean-bag chair that gave me a good look at the two rooms where she did most of her living.

The front room was depressing enough, with its sprung worn couch, two garish orange bean-bag chairs and black velvet painting of a brave Indian warrior who looked as if he'd spent some time in Las Vegas, but the dining room was even worse. All it contained was a collection of cardboard boxes piled haphazardly wall-to-wall. A skinny calico kitten sat on top of the boxes watching me. She was one of the very few kittens I'd ever seen who looked unhappy.

"I'm moving in a couple of weeks," Patricia Moore explained as she plopped herself down on the couch across from me.

The only light came from a small table with a buff blue shade that had several stains on it.

This place made Gilhooley's look like a cover subject for the next *Good Housekeeping*.

"I'm moving, that's why the mess. I mean, I'm a slob but not *that* much of one." She hit on her beer and then smiled. "I'm gonna do exactly what my mama always told me *not* to do."

"What's that?"

"Rodeo. Lot of Indian girls dream of that. They see all these sexy Indian guys ridin' broncs at rodeos and fall in love with 'em. First time I ran away with a rodeo guy I was fourteen."

"I'll bet that didn't make your mother too happy."

"Are you kidding? She done a lot worse things than that when she was young. I mean, I loved her and all but I didn't have no illusions about her." Sad smile. "Plus, her and my Aunt Karen, they got all the looks." Shook her head. "Fucking Rhodes, anyway. He killed them both."

She started crying. No warning. Full, angry tears. "And then that bastard goes and cuts off their noses, too."

"Why would he do that?"

She looked up, enraged. "If you've come here to defend him, mister, you can sashay your ass right out my door."

"I'm not defending him. I just want to know why he would have killed them."

"Because they had somethin' on him, Mom and Aunt Karen did, and he was afraid they'd tell somebody." Then, "You mind if I turn on the TV?"

"It's your place."

"I just feel better when the TV's on. I can't explain it, I just do."

She punched the button on the remote control; a color image of a country and western singer filled the screen. She put her head back momentarily, closed her eyes, listened.

"Patty?"

"Uh-huh."

"Why would he want to kill them?"

She was pretty drunk. Her eyes were still closed.

"I used to have a boyfriend named Running Fox," she murmured, without moving. "When we was in high school, he asked me to marry him—and you know what I did?"

"What?"

"Run off with a rodeo rider again."

"And that finished you with Running Fox?"

"Uh-huh. He wasn't even pissed. He was just real, real hurt and I felt like shit about it but no matter what I did, he wouldn't take me back. You know what he's doin' today?"

"Huh-uh."

"He's a doctor. Surgeon."

I wasn't sure what to say.

"I seen his wife once."

"Running Fox's?"

"Uh-huh."

"Nice-looking?"

"Gorgeous."

She brought her face down and stared at me. "My mom and David . . .?"

"Yeah?"

"I don't know why they hated each other so much, but they really did. I seen him throw her up against the wall one night and slap her. I thought he was gonna kill her."

"This was where?"

"Right here. This apartment."

"But you don't know what it was about?"

She shook her head. "She wouldn't tell me and he wouldn't either. This state should have the death penalty."

"A lot of people seem to think so."

"Somebody should kill that bastard."

Her reverie had given her thoughts and voice a temporary clarity but now she was sliding back into the bottle. And she was also getting groggy.

"I appreciate your time."

I wasn't going to learn anything else here tonight. I stood up.

"I used to sleep with David. While he was still living with Cindy, I mean. You mention my name to her and she'll tell you I'm just some rummy old whore."

David certainly got around.

"I wasn't good enough for him, though, you know that? He'd never take me any place in public. He was ashamed of me except when he was drunk and he'd sneak up here. I always wanted to tell Cindy, just to watch her face."

"Well," I said, wanting to leave, "good luck with your move."

Then she surprised me. Her head fell against the back of the chair again. This time she was snoring.

SEVEN

10:00 P.M.

There was a hard wind whipping up silty silver dust outside the police station. Clouds covered the moon and you could taste rain on the chilling air.

Not that the posse was deterred. That's how they thought of themselves, I'm sure. A posse right out of a pulp magazine where a guy with a flinty face and a white hat pumps bullets into a guy with a grizzled face and a black hat.

Three pick-up trucks, each with a shotgun rack in the back, and the radio tuned to a right-wing radio show.

The buildings on Main Street were all dark except for the furious light and noise of the two taverns—one neon Bud, one neon Coors—sitting like bookends on either end of the street. Down a few doors, two stone lions and two stone gargoyles decorating the front of the tiny Carnegie-grant library sat watching us all with a kind of weary contempt. Generations of human folly had been played out before them.

During the first day, yesterday, the Highway Patrol had lent a helicopter, and several other smalltown police departments had lent officers. But now it was back to business so Chief Gibbs had to use some locals.

By the looks of them, he couldn't have been too happy about it. The men had beer guts and cowboy boots and big silver belt buckles and beery crazed eyes. There had always been types like them, eager for blood and lynching, as far back as the Bronze Age and as recently as 1964, when a few dozen brave men hunted down three civil-rights workers and castrated and killed them. Interesting to know what political commentator Rush Limbaugh would have had to say about that.

Chief Gibbs was giving them orders. The posse looked bored.

"You've all got cellulars. That's why I got them for you. You see him, you call me. You don't shoot. You got that?"

"What happens if he shoots at us first?" one of them said.

"Then you shoot back. But only," Gibbs said, "if he shoots first."

The door opened behind him and two deputies, including the chunky one who'd been operating the radio on the other night, came out.

They wore uniforms and jackets and badges and bore shotguns. Their heads were angled away from the whipping wind. Raindrops bit like gnats on my face now.

"Where the hell they goin'?" one of the truck-driving men said.

"With you."

"You didn't say nothin' 'bout no deputies," objected another.

"You sure as hell didn't think I was going to let you three boys go out there alone, did you?"

One of the men smirked. "Clarence here gonna give us orders, is he?"

I would have felt sorry for Clarence—his roly-polyness cast him as the most incompetent boy at Scout Camp—but I couldn't forget his meanness towards Cindy.

"He's an official deputy and you're not," Chief Gibbs said.

Clarence held a pudgy hand up to the sky. "It's raining."

"Hey, no shit," one of the men said. "Clarence said it's raining."

The other two sniggered.

"You'll be fine," Chief Gibbs said to his nephew. "Little rain shouldn't slow you down. If you had the dogs, that'd be another matter." He looked at the three men. "You have any questions?"

"Yeah, how come Clarence is such a dork?" one of them said.

The other deputy, who looked snake-quick and snake-mean, said, "You boys keep this shit up, they're gonna find one of you dead in a ditch by morning. You understand?"

They changed then, the way bullies do whenever they meet a more formidable bully. There were some momentary smirks and quick glances but they knew better than to push it.

"I guess I don't need to remind you boys that Tom Rand here was Green Beret in 'Nam, and that he broke both of Spider MacAtee's arms the night Spider cut up his wife," Gibbs said. "And since Clarence and Tom are cousins, and since Tom has always sorta stuck up for Clarence, he will be real, real pissed off if any of you boys hassle Clarence in any way whatsoever, if you catch my drift. You catch my drift?"

He was addressing the tallest of the three, the one with the Hank Williams Jr. T-shirt.

Rand said, "You catch his drift, Slocum?"

Slocum had to decide whether to look weak in front of his pals or risk Rand's temper which seemed, just from looking at the guy, psychotic.

"I catch his drift," Slocum said.

"Good," Gibbs said. "Then we won't have any problems tonight, now will we?"

Over a cup of hot, bitter coffee in his office, I listened as Gibbs said, "The good ones—the family men and the decent men and the law-abiding men—they'll go out during the day to hunt for Rhodes, but at night they want to be home with their wife and kids so that's when you end up with the hill-billies and the rednecks. Kinda like huntin' squirrel to them, except here they just might get a chance to shoot an actual human being, which tickles the shit out of them."

"No idea where he is so far?"

"Not a clue."

"Maybe he got away."

Gibbs shook his head. "Indians don't run. I know you're not supposed to generalize about a group of people like that, but they don't. For one thing, there's really no place for an Indian to run to, when you think about it. Full-blooded the way Rhodes is, he'd get spotted pretty easy in truckstops and places like that. And for another thing, nobody knows this land like the Indians do. Rhodes will know a hundred places to hide I never heard of—and they're all within five, ten miles of town."

"How's Cindy doing?"

"Not so good. She went out with the search party this morning. She's afraid somebody's gonna kill him. And they probably will if they get half a chance."

"You think she's home?"

"Could be. And it'd be nice if you stopped by and saw her. She needs some friends right now. Her being a deputy and all—well, she isn't real popular with either Indians or whites sometimes. She's a lonely gal."

"But a good one."

He nodded. "The best, you ask me. I mean, I don't like to think of myself as a racist but I can take Indians or leave them. Met some good ones, met some bad ones. I just don't want you to think I like Cindy because she's some type of affirmative-action gal or something. She's the best deputy I ever had—except maybe for Rand, and the thing he's best at is keeping people in line—and also one of the most decent. In her time off, she's out at the reservation making sure all those little kids are getting their booster shots and things like that. And on Saturdays, she's out there tutoring kids in reading and math. Her people are finally starting to succeed. They're becoming very sharp at business and farming and learning how to capitalize on their heritage, and it's all because of people like Cindy.''

"That's quite a speech.''

The Chief smiled. "Meant every word of it.''

"Clarence doesn't seem to like her.''

He smiled again. "That's because she's a whole lot smarter, prettier and tougher than Clarence.''

"Don't let him hear you say that.''

"His mother died of liver cancer ten, twelve years ago—my sister, God rest her soul—and Clarence has kinda been my charge ever since. His old man, who I always thought was a no-good drunken sonofabitch and who up and walked out on them just a few months before Bernice got sick, anyway his old man hated Indians and I'm afraid it rubbed off on Clarence.''

I took the last of my coffee. "You ever know Sandra Moore's daughter?''

"Oh, yeah.''

"I spent a little time with her tonight.''

"She's just about as pathetic as her mother. The Indians have a real hard time with the bottle.''

"You know any reason her mother and David Rhodes would hate each other so much?''

"Sure.''

"Sure? Just like that?''

"David's sister was kidnapped from the reservation when she was six years old.''

"Right.''

"Well, guess who was supposed to be babysitting her that day?''

"Sandra Moore?''

"Right. She still came back to the reservation occasionally in those days."

"No wonder, then."

"David got in some trouble with the Cedar Rapids PD a couple of times because he'd get drunk and go up to Sandra's and hassle her. Plus, Sandra had a way of putting on airs. Even when she was living on the reservation, she was working for the Hestons and trying to give all her friends the impression she was a lot better than they were."

"She was working for the Hestons and still doing babysitting jobs here?"

Gibbs shrugged. "Not 'jobs.' But she and David's mother were good friends. She just said she'd watch the little girl while David's mother drove to Des Moines. Cedar Rapids or Des Moines, those are the two big cities to people who live here." He grinned. "Not exactly New York or Los Angeles but good enough to get by on, I guess."

I stood up, offered my hand, thanked him for the coffee. "Guess I'll go see Cindy."

"Know where she lives?"

"Yeah."

"Make her laugh a little. She needs that."

"I'll do my best."

EIGHT

Dear Mr. Payne,

I've changed my mind. I'd like to go flying at 10:00 A.M. tomorrow.

Sincerely,
Silver Moon

Cindy Rhodes was not at home so I'd come back to my motel and was about to put the key in my lock when I saw the note that had been taped to the door.

I smiled as I read it. Given her fear of flying, this was a major decision for Silver Moon.

Then I heard the noise from inside.

The first thing I thought of was the pig. I couldn't recall his name at that moment—you have to say a pig's name several times before it sticks in your mind—but I could picture him cavorting about inside my room.

But what if it wasn't the pig?

I'd irritated a number of people in and around the reservation the past few days. What if one of them had decided to irritate me right back?

I took out my Ruger.

I don't do that very often.

I believe in the advice I got at Quantico: if you draw your gun, you're likely to use it, and if you use it, it's probably because you used your emotions instead of your head.

I'd always cherished that piece of advice and quoted it whenever I wanted to rattle the more macho types of lawmen I encountered.

In fact, I quoted it to myself as I eased the key in and turned it, then pushed the door inward and stepped inside.

And all the time I quoted it, I kept my Ruger in my hand. No sense in taking chances.

"Please don't turn on the light."

I'd found Cindy.

"Are you all right?"

"Yes. But I'd prefer the darkness if you don't mind."

"Fine with me."

"Be careful so you don't trip."

"Thanks, Mom."

She laughed. "No wonder David thinks I'm such a pain in the ass. I was always the older sister, always watching out for all the little kids."

"I thought it was kind of sweet, warning me."

"Do you plan to put that gun away any time soon?"

"How about right now?"

"Right now would be great."

I put the Ruger away and made my way through the deep and shifting shadows. I smelled hand soap, mildew, furniture polish, dust and heat.

There were two armchairs collected around a battered table. She sat in one, I sat in the other.

"How're you doing?" I said.

"I need to see him."

"Maybe they'll find him."

"Even if they find him, I won't see him. Not ever again."

"They won't kill him."

"But he'll be in prison."

"Oh."

"It'll kill him, being in prison."

"We can find him a good lawyer. If you say he didn't do it—"

"That's just it," she said in the darkness.

"What is?"

"Maybe he did do it."

"Oh."

"That's what I'm afraid of, anyway."

We didn't talk, not for a long time, just listened to the crickets and the big trucks out on the highway, and the occasional teenager with his powerful car and even more powerful radio.

"You know the funny thing?" she whispered.

"What?"

"We haven't made love for two years."

"I'm sorry."

"I don't think he finds me appealing anymore. I'm sort of like his sister. Did that ever happen with your wife?"

"No. I loved my wife. She was my life."

"And you never got tired of her sexually?"

"No."

"Did you ever get tired of a woman sexually?"

I laughed gently. "I don't think so. First of all, I haven't been to bed with that many women. And second of all, I was always sort of grateful when they went to bed with me. I'm not exactly Robert Redford. And besides, every woman I went to bed with taught me something."

"You mean sexually?"

"Sure, sexually—how to be a better lover, you know, more dutiful and less worried about my own pleasures. But they also taught me more about women. In the long run, they were teaching me how to be a better husband to the woman I'd marry someday—and not just sexually. In every way, I mean."

"I envy your wife. It must've been a nice marriage."

"It sure was for me. And I think it was for her."

"You shouldn't put your looks down. You're nice-looking."

"But not exactly Robert Redford."

"Do you think he killed those women?"

"I don't think it can be ruled out."

"I love him so much."

"I know."

"And I'm so lonely. That's what's so strange. I'm so afraid for him and he's all I can think of, and yet I feel so lonely, too." She paused. "Would you just lie down with me?"

"Sure."

"I think that's why I came here."

"That's fine. Lying down with you will be a pleasure."

"I don't want to make love."

"That's all right."

"Really?"

"Really," I said.

"I think that's why I came here. I mean, I didn't admit it to myself, but that's why I came here."

"Would you like to lie down first?"

"Now I'm scared."

"Nothing to be scared of."

"And I feel like a slut."

I laughed at her and found her hand in the shadows. Her

skin was smooth and her hand surprisingly small, like a girl's.
"I don't think you have to worry about being a slut."

"I really don't want to make love."

"I know."

"I just need to be held."

"That sounds nice."

"Would you mind lying down first?"

"No problem."

I got up and went over and took off my nylon jacket and
laid down on my side on the bed. The springs squeaked and
the wooden headboard banged once against the wall.

I stood up again. "Let me pull the bed out from the wall
a little."

I pulled it out and laid down again.

"I just feel so self-conscious now."

"Better hurry before I fall asleep."

She laughed. "That was a good one."

Then suddenly she was up and coming across the small
space between chair and bed. And lying down on her side
facing me.

"Is my breath bad?" she asked.

"Not from here anyway."

"Can I breathe on you and test it out?"

"Sure."

She breathed on me and tested it out.

"It's fine. Now relax."

"Don't try to hold me right away, all right? I mean, I'm
still a little nervous."

"So am I."

"Really?"

"Sure. You think I let strange women do stuff like this to
me all the time?"

She laughed again. "You're crazy and I really like that."

"Thank you."

Then, "He called me tonight."

"I figured he would sometime."

"I asked him where he was but he wouldn't tell me."

"Oh."

"You know what I'm afraid of?"

"What?"

But before she answered, she took my free arm—my other was propping up my head—and placed it on her hip. Her hip felt very, very nice.

"What I'm afraid of is that I'll help him."

"Without telling Chief Gibbs?"

"Right. And it'll all be over, then. My whole life. I'll lose my job because I helped him. I was one of the first ones from the reservation to go to college. I didn't finish but I went for nearly three years, and—"

"It wouldn't be worth it."

"I know."

"You need to think about it."

"But if he calls—"

"Tell him to turn himself in. Tell him you can't help him."

"I keep seeing him as a little boy. He was the cutest little boy I've ever seen. I always hoped we could have a son of our own and that he'd look just like David. God, I must've had a crush on him when I was four years old."

And then the rain started and we just lay there side by side and listened to it on the roof and smelled it through the open window, two prairie creatures dry and safe from the night.

And then she said, "Would you mind holding me?"

"If you insist."

"I do."

"I'm glad you do."

"But nothing else."

"I know."

"I really appreciate this."

"So do I."

"Your wife was lucky."

"No," I said. "I was the lucky one, believe me."

And then I drew her to me, gently, tenderly there in the darkness, and she smelled and felt of woman, friend and lover and sister, and then she started softly crying and her warm tears on my face were both sad and erotic.

> *Even in many prisons, the red man was treated as an*
> *outcast. He was frequently brutalized by both the*
> *guards and other prisoners, and was often sold as*
> *cheap labor to private industry by corrupt wardens.*
>   Professor David Cromwell's Indian Journal

Autumn came.

Anna had followed the stout, handsome Douglas Ashlock virtually every night. He had his card games at the country club, his business meetings at City Hall, and his carousing nights at three different downtown drinking establishments.

He never once went to Gray House.

One Saturday afternoon, just as the leaves were turning, Anna borrowed Mrs. Goldman's buggy and went out into the countryside. The fall leaves were almost blinding in their beauty. The hills smelled of smoky perfumes.

Gray House was unimaginably lovely.

All Anna could think of were the splendid Victorian homes she'd seen in magazines about London, everyone inside all genteel and elegant.

Gray House was surrounded by a black iron fence.

No signs of life were visible.

She thought of Poe's *The Fall of the House of Usher* and of its powerful opening description of a house that seemed barren of all life.

She pulled the buggy up to the front and checked the black iron gates. Padlocked.

Anna would not see any more of Gray House on this particular day.

One day in the library, Anna came across it by pure accident.

Looking through the London *Times*, a newspaper she'd read ever since Jack the Ripper had gotten her interested in British society, she saw a headline on page 5. "CIRCLE OF

SIX" MEMBERS ARRESTED. *"Six House of Lords members 'groom' young slum girls to give them pleasure,"* the text read. *"A vile and degenerate plot" notes Scotland Yard Inspector.*

Anna read the entire story in horror and disbelief. Now she knew what Douglas Ashlock's "secret society"—which Trace had innocently mentioned one night—really meant.

"I need to say something to you, Anna."

"I think I know what you're going to say, Trace."

"Maybe it's time I started seeing other girls."

"Maybe it is."

"I have needs, Anna."

"I understand, Trace."

"There are several girls over at the soda fountain who seem to like me just fine."

"I'm sure they do."

"'And they're cute girls, too."

"I'm sure they are."

"Oh God, Anna, I don't mean any of this. I'm just trying to scare you."

"Can't we just go out and hold hands like we used to?"

"I don't think I can do that, Anna."

"Your needs."

"You don't need to be sarcastic about my needs."

"I'm not being sarcastic, Trace. I know you have needs."

"Maybe we should get married."

"Two minutes ago you were telling me you wanted to go out with these cute girls at the soda fountain."

"I didn't say I wanted to go out with them. I said they wanted to go out with me."

"Oh God, Trace, I can't argue anymore. And that's all we do these days. Argue."

"Well, it's not unreasonable for a modern young man to have certain expectations of a modern young girl in this day and age."

"I don't think I'm all that modern and I think that's the problem."

"Yes," Trace said miserably, "I think that's *exactly* the problem."

INITIAL CRIME REPORT

Cedar Rapids, Iowa   Case Number: ___ 91-12-0056

Offense: ___ Homicide ___

Victim: ___ Jane Doe NA/F ___   DOB: ___ 02-14-51

Location: ___ 904 Birch Road ___   Time: ___ 2330 Hours

Means: ___ Unknown ___

Weapon: ___ Unknown ___

Details: ___
Reporting officer arrived at 904 Birch Road at 2330 in response to anonymous phone
call about a human female arm being discovered near the burned-out mansion. When
I arrived I found a cardboard box (which the caller had described) with a) the arm
underneath and b) a dog locked in the garage.

R/o stayed at scene and awaited arrival of detectives. Case was then turned over to
Detective Andrea Long. On orders from Detective Long, R/o remained at scene to
keep back onlookers.

signature

NINE

I spent most of the following morning in Cindy's office going through the crime-scene data that the Cedar Rapids police had given Chief Gibbs to compare with his data from the first mutilation murder.

The supplemental crime reports showed that the Cedar Rapids people had done a very thorough job.

But for all of it—and the evidence list ran to more than thirty pages—what made me most curious was the fact that on both victims, the sister a week earlier, not only had the nose been mutilated but the arm had been cut off.

I wasn't sure why, but that particular method of operation sounded familiar to me.

Evidence List

96-8-0056-M1: yellow blouse from victim's body

96-8-0056-M2: white bra from victim's body

96-8-0056-M3: combings from victim's pubic
hair

96-8-0056-M4: washings from victim's vagina

96-8-0056-M5: scrapings from under victim's
fingernails, right hand

96-8-0056-M6: scrapings from under victim's
fingernails, left hand

96-8-0056-M7: combings from victim's hair

_____
signature

I was using Cindy's office so I decided to link up her computer with mine.

The process took fifteen minutes and at the end of it I was able to find material relating to the ritual mutilations by certain Indian tribes during their wars with each other and with white men.

> * Each Indian tribe had its own way of
> slashing and thereby "marking" the arms
> and legs of its victims.

* Indian warriors followed a practice called "counting coup"—touching a live or dead enemy and then crying out, "I claim it"—meaning "I claim this brave's body and soul." This sometimes led to ritualistic slashing, in addition to the inevitable death.

* Some tribes believed that by cutting off the limb of an enemy, you maimed his soul as well as his body . . . leaving him less than whole in the Afterworld.

I then punched up some additional information.

* Sex murders are typically stabbings, strangulations or beatings.

* If the killer used a weapon he brought along, this points to an organized person.

* If the killer used whatever weapon was available, this points to a disorganized personality.

But as I read through several pages of material on post-offense behavior I kept thinking back to the notation that certain Plains Indians had severed the limbs of fallen warriors in order to ensure that the warriors would be maimed in the Afterworld.

For some nagging reason, this sounded familiar.

Had I heard of a case like this before?

A few minutes later, I was talking to a friend of mine in Quantico.

"Say again," he said.

"Cuts off a limb so that in the Afterworld, that person will be maimed. Can you remember a case like that?"

"No."

"How about Native Americans in general?"

"That's where I'll start, Payne, but I'll tell you, I'm so busy right now I can't guarantee when I can get back to you."

"Fine."

"How's Iowa?"

"Iowa's great as always."

"Man, you sure love that state."

"I sure do. The countryside more than the cities but the cities are all right, too."

"I'll do what I can for you on this."

"I appreciate it."

"*Ciao.*"

"*Ciao*? A Bureau guy saying *Ciao*?"

He laughed. "I knew I could get you going with that."

Cindy came in ten minutes later with a crisp new khaki uniform and a worn tired face. Not much sleep after leaving my motel room, apparently. She looked pretty and sad in a way that was touching, in a way that made me want to hold her again in the quietly erotic embrace of last night.

"You mind if I close this door?" she said.

"Huh-uh."

She closed the door. "I'm sorry about last night."

"Yes, I guess you did sort of take me against my will."

She didn't smile. "I'm a married woman."

"There's married and there's married, Cindy. You shouldn't feel guilty about it. I needed to be with somebody and so did you."

"I feel like a slut." Her brown eyes were slick with tears.

"It was tender and gentle and fun," I said. "And you're one hell of a decent person. And one hell of a long way from being a slut."

"He's running for his life and I'm sleeping with somebody."

"He didn't worry about you a whole lot when you needed him."

"It shouldn't have happened. And it was my fault as much as yours. I just wanted you to know that."

I decided to change the subject and almost immediately wished I hadn't. "He try to call you last night after you got home?"

"No."

She was lying.

I could see it right there in her beautiful brown gaze. She was a very moral person, Cindy was, and lying, like sleeping around guiltlessly, just wasn't in her.

But I wasn't going to say anything.

It wasn't my place.

She nodded to the front of the station. "They brought the tracking dogs back this morning."

"You going with them?"

"I'm going to look a few places on my own."

"I see."

"Chief Gibbs said it was all right to do it so I thought why not. Right?"

"Right."

Obviously she knew just where he was hiding and was going out there the moment she got a chance.

"You want me to go with you?" I asked.

"Better not. In case I run into him."

"I see."

She touched her hand to the doorknob.

"You remember what you said last night about not blowing your whole life—everything you've worked so hard for—to help David?"

"Yeah, I guess I remember that."

"Keep that in mind."

"Are you implying that I know where he's hiding?"

"I'm not implying anything, Cindy. I just don't want you to get into trouble."

She surprised me by walking three steps over to my chair and kissing me tenderly on the mouth.

"You were nice and gentle, and I appreciate that," she said.

"I should be the appreciative one, Cindy. You're a fine

woman. Being with you was an honor. I don't think you know
just how fine a person you really are.''

I'd embarrassed her. She went back to the door. ''Maybe
I'll check in on you tonight. See how things are going. Just
to have dinner or something.''

''I'd like that.''

She stared at me a long moment then, and was gone.

TEN

"She didn't want to tell you."

"Tell me what?"

"She's wearing diapers."

"Ah."

"She's afraid all the excitement will get to her so she asked me if she could have one of mine."

"That was nice of you."

"You be safe now."

"I will. I promise."

"That little gal is my whole life. Always has been. I took care of her all through the Depression—she was always a sick little girl—but ever since, she's been taking care of me."

The kind of love he was expressing was something we

don't see enough of on this weary old planet—pure, gracious, selfless. He'd given me a glimpse of them as children—I could see them in their Indian attire—and then as adults surviving one marriage each (neither had had any children) and then having a kind of pseudo-marriage together as sister and brother.

She sat in the rear cockpit of the plane now in her Snoopy helmet and goggles, all ready to go.

"We'll be fine, Iron Crow."

"Can I go say goodbye to her one more time?"

I made a face. "I'm sorry. No more visits permitted."

He looked horrified.

"I'm kidding, Iron Crow. Of course you can say goodbye to her."

He raised a beautiful Red Indian blanket he had laid across his right arm.

We walked through the buffalo grass. You could smell autumn again on the late-morning air. The sky was almost cloudless and in the hills to the west an ancient red Ford tractor was playing the cornfields.

"How're you doing, Sis?" Iron Crow said.

"I'm not as scared as I was all night." She turned her Snoopy helmet and dusky goggles in my direction. "I couldn't sleep at all. I kept thinking that I was going to fall out of the plane."

"Silver Moon, you really don't have to go, you know," Iron Crow said. "Payne here won't mind."

"I sure won't, Silver Moon. You just do what makes you comfortable."

"I want to be able to talk about it at dinner tonight," she said. And then grinned with her gleaming store-boughts. "And at a lot of dinners the rest of my life."

I smiled. "That seems reasonable."

"You eat dinner with the same people night after night," Iron Crow said, "it's nice to have something new to talk about once in a while."

"But if I start screaming," Silver Moon said.

"Yes?" I said.

"Will you take me down right away?"

"That's a deal. You start screaming, we come down right away."

"Maybe I'll enjoy myself," she said, utter terror narrowing her eyes and freezing her lips.

"I sure enjoyed myself," Iron Crow said, "and I didn't wet myself until after we came down."

She shot him a warning glance that I was sure had to do with the diapers I wasn't supposed to know about.

"Well, you ready?"

She glanced, horrified, at her brother.

He took the blanket and spread it over her legs and knees and then he leaned in and kissed her.

"You'll like it, Sis."

"I hope so."

"Just think of how jealous Running Deer will be when you tell her."

"That's true."

"So just relax."

"I'll try."

"And just keep your eyes squinched closed till you're up there. Going up and coming down are the scary parts, Sis. The rest is a lot of fun."

"I'm squinching my eyes shut right now," she said. But you couldn't see anything behind her smoky goggles.

"She's all yours, Payne," Iron Crow said. I wasn't sure if he meant his sister or the plane. Or both.

The gods of the air decided to give Silver Moon a little scare. They do stuff like that sometimes, like mischievous children who want to remind you of their existence.

We bucked some rough headwinds before we found some nice smooth going up over the piney hills.

I noted that she hadn't screamed yet, not even when we'd been fighting the headwinds.

"How're you doing?" I shouted back to her.

"This is the most wonderful experience of my life!"

This happens sometimes. People who hate to fly actually

get up there and they don't want to come down. Of course, just as often, it happens the other way, too. People who hate to fly start begging you to take them down after only a few minutes.

We looked over the Grant Wood colors, red of barn, green of cornfield, fast dark blue of river, black-and-white of dairy cows, mahogany of horses in the hills, cool and deep shadow of forest, burnished gold of limestone cliffs.

Every few minutes, she'd shout, "I love this, Mr. Payne! I love this!"

She was sure going to have a lot of good new material for her friends.

We were just swooping down near the old dam, where a woman in red shorts and a white halter and summer-blonde hair was fishing from a battered green rowboat, when I saw, to the east along a mile stretch of gravel road running parallel to the river, Cindy Rhodes' personal car, a brown Dodge station wagon, traveling at a high rate of speed.

The Dodge wagon came to a T-intersection and then turned west. I had a terrible feeling that I knew what she was doing.

Silver Moon leaned forward and tapped me on the shoulder. "You know how I said I didn't want you to try any fancy tricks?"

"Uh-huh."

"Well, how about if you tried just one, just a real little one."

The sweetness she shared with her brother should be bottled and each of us, every man, woman and child on the planet, should partake of the fabulous elixir at least once a day.

"I'll do a real little one."

A sort of half-roll is what I did, the nice gentle tailwinds helping a lot, nothing spooky, just one more thing for Silver Moon to talk about.

"Would you do that one more time?" she said when I was done.

I laughed and did it again.

At the same time, I noticed the brown Dodge had pulled off the gravel road into some deep woods.

Cindy, in her khaki uniform, got out of the wagon and started into the trees. She was soon lost in shadow.

She was, I suspected, about to throw her life away, the life she'd built so carefully, so proudly for herself.

"Mr. Payne?" Silver Moon said when I came out of the half-roll.

"Uh-huh?"

"Just one more time. Please? Just one more time?"

ELEVEN

In 1773, a man named Peter Pond came all the way from Connecticut to Ioway Territory to try his luck at making a fortune in the fur trade. Pond left a journal and it's quite a good one, filled with images of bark canoes laden with blankets, cloth, guns and powder that he and his companions hoped to trade with the Indians for buffalo hides, beaver, fox, and otter skins.

Seventeen days into their journey, Pond wrote down what may have been the new country's first "fish" story, though he got three men to sign his journal and testify to its veracity. Pond claimed that he caught three catfish weighing, respectively, seventy-five pounds, one hundred pounds and one hundred and four pounds. As Pond noted (in his most peculiar spelling), the fish fed twelve very hungry men and ''Thay all Declared that they felt the Better for The Meale. Nor did I perseave that Eney of Them were Sick or Complained.''

I always remember Pond whenever I'm out in the deeper forest because he felt an affinity for the shifting shadows and sweet scents and myriad life-forms you find in the woods—an affinity that bordered on the religious. ''Worlds unto Their Own,'' as he remarks at one point. ''And the Breath of God Hisself Sweet and Cool on yer back.''

The woods surrounding the cabin where David Rhodes was holed up were nearly as sweet, shadowy and swarming with life, seen and unseen, as Pond had known them.

What always struck me about forests this deep—wild plum and wild cherry and box-elder and soft maple and Virginia creeper; walnuts and hackberries and cottonwoods and bur oak and steep clay ridges—was that some of it pre-dated even the dinosaurs of sixty-five million years ago. If that doesn't make you think about a cosmic creator of some kind, nothing ever will.

I came up over a grassy ridge on my haunches and down below, in a valley of prairie flowers giving way to prairie grasses now that late summer was upon us, there sat a crude wooden cabin that had been painted turd-brown.

All the shades were drawn. No radio, no TV played. Insects were loud in the stillness and rabbits thumped and thrashed in the long grasses nearby. Afternoon's shadows were deepening, tainted with the purple of coming dusk.

I was on a simple mission.

Or maybe not so simple, otherwise why would I not only have brought my Ruger along but have it in my right hand, ready?

A few scenarios played furtively through my mind: Cindy had come to the cabin door and he'd killed her and fled, hence the drawn shades and silence; Cindy had decided to capture him herself, getting him into her car before any other cops could hassle him; man and wife, they'd taken off together. In a fast car, Mexico was just two days away.

I started down into the valley, Ruger ready, winding my

way through a steep stand of cedars and oaks, keeping a constant eye on the side window of the cabin for any sign of movement inside. Maybe they really were gone.

The closer I got to the cabin, the more evidence I found of teenagers using the place as a rendezvous point: rusty beer cans and Trojan packs that looked like red cut flowers, tiny insect-like marijuana roaches and pop bottles broken to saber-like points, and crumpled cigarette packs that dew had stained piss-yellow.

A voice. Female. Inside the cabin.

Not loud. Not anxious. Under control, even soft, but just loud enough to carry on the same breeze that also lofted the red-shouldered hawks I'd seen earlier.

Cindy. Talking. Voice through the screen.

Crouching, I ran across the clearing to the oak tree that stood at an angle to the front door. Only one way in and that was it.

I would have to assume two things. One, that the cabin door would be unlocked and two, that I could get through the door before David Rhodes—or Cindy, depending on her mood—could draw down on me.

I was uncomfortably sweaty and it wasn't from the heat; the temperature was in the low seventies. Mine was the sweat of anxiety. I could get killed, I could alienate Cindy for ever. I didn't want to keep on thinking about last night but I couldn't help it. I hadn't tasted such sweet warm breath since the death of my wife, or felt such tender yearning breasts, or dozed and dreamt so comfortably afterward in the darkness. I had this obtrusive crush on her and I felt as awkward and untutored as a fourteen-year-old.

I ran across the clearing between tree and door.

I raised my foot, cop-style, kicked once hard at a spot just below the doorknob.

And charged forward—hoping that the big wooden slab of door would oblige me by popping inward.

The door slapped backward against the wall. A scream. A deeper voice, cursing.

I went through the doorway.

A snapshot: Rhodes in a straight-backed wooden chair at a small wooden table, reaching for his gun. Cindy grabbing a coffee pot to hurl it at me. They froze this way just long enough for me to get inside and impress on them the fact that I held a gun and they didn't.

"You sonofabitch," Rhodes said.

"Just stay where you are."

"Robert . . ." Cindy said.

"I want you out of here," I said.

She looked startled. "What?"

"Out of here. Back in town." I came deeper into the cabin. It appeared as if the Salvation Army had stopped by one day and unloaded some furniture they'd had in the basement for many long and dark years. The frayed plump couch and matching frayed armchair smelled of mildew and rot; the shaggy blue throw rug on the floor stank of animal urine of some kind. In one corner, there was a sink with rusty streaks down its white back, and a hotplate on the counter next to it. Two cans of Campbells tomato soup stood empty.

"What the hell are you talking about, Payne?" he said.

"Why take her down with you, Rhodes? You've never done a damned thing for her. Why not let her go back to town so Gibbs won't know she was helping you."

"What I do is my business," Cindy said.

Rhodes said, "He's right."

He surprised me and I sensed he also surprised Cindy. You didn't expect such largesse from a man like Rhodes.

"You go back to town, Cindy," David said.

"Don't listen to him, David. This isn't any of his business."

Rhodes shook his head. He looked older today, and tired, his gaunt handsome face strained with worry. He sat in his straight-backed chair, shoulders slouched, a beaten man.

"Go on, Cindy. Now," he said.

She glared at me then looked back at him. "I don't want to go, David. I want to be here with you. I can help you get a car and get out of here."

She went over and sat down on the edge of the day bed,

the only place to sleep, except for the floor, in the cabin. If he looked old, she looked young, very young and sad and lost.

She said, quietly, "We didn't finish talking, David. This is the first good talk we've had in years."

He stared at her a long time. "You heard me, Cindy. I want you to go."

"You sonofabitch," she said to me. "You had no right to come here and do this to us."

I wasn't sure what to feel. Things had been so simple when I'd been outside the cabin. Rhodes was a bad guy and Cindy his naive victim and I her knight in slightly tarnished armor. I would rescue the damsel. But things hadn't worked out quite the way I'd hoped.

Now I was an intruder, and a callous one, and I saw that whatever tenderness we'd shared in the lonely darkness last night had been furtive at best. She was in every respect, good and bad, right and wrong, in love with this man. I felt ridiculously betrayed, as if a few moments in the rainy shadows of a motel room had given me some kind of spiritual claim on her.

Now I really was an intruder.

I needed to hate Rhodes pure and clean, and I tried to, too.

I told myself that he had escaped from police custody, that he had never done a damned thing for this wife of his here, and that he was most likely the killer of at least two women.

But that didn't help any.

He was sad and she was sad and now I was sad, and we were all together in this tiny sunless mildew-smelling cabin and it didn't seem to matter if he was a killer or if she was going to lose her job. We were just three people who knew only one thing—that what lay ahead was likely very, very bad.

"Go on, Cindy. Please." He looked old; and now he sounded old, too.

"You don't have to do what he says, David."

He raised his eyes to hers. I sensed he was about to cry.

"I've done things, Cindy—things you don't know about—things you'd hate me for if you knew."

"Don't say any more, David. Not in front of him."

"I'm not exaggerating, Cindy. If you knew the things I'd done . . ."

"Why don't you go, Cindy?" I said. "Somebody might have spotted you here and told Gibbs, and—"

"You think I give a damn about that? That's your white-man bullshit. Worry about the job, worry about being respectable. They're going to kill him, or haven't you figured that out yet, Payne?"

She went over, knelt down next to him. Her knees cracked in the stillness.

She took his hand, smoothed it across her lovely cheek.

She set his hand down on hers, then, and she said to me, "One or two men in that posse, they'd just love to kill an Indian and that's just what they'll try to do with David."

"You go back to town," I said. "I promise I won't let that happen."

She laughed bitterly. "Do you know how pontifical you sound, Payne? The Great White Father! 'I promise I won't let that happen.' This isn't the FBI, Payne. This is a small town with a lot of people who hate Indians and who now have a half-ass excuse to kill one in cold blood."

"I'll call Gibbs. I'll tell him to come out alone."

"It could still happen." She had a child's terror at that moment, an image of death so compelling that she couldn't let go of it.

"He's right," Rhodes said. "I'll be fine." He leaned down and kissed her gently on the mouth.

The intruder, I looked away.

"I've treated you like shit all my life and I'm sorry, Cindy, I really am."

And then he was crying.

She held him and let him cry and after a time I went to the door and opened it and stepped outside so I wouldn't have to intrude so much. I had both their guns stuffed into my belt. They weren't going anywhere.

I gave them ten minutes and sometime during it, Cindy started crying, too, and I had a sense of what wives visiting husbands on Death Row must sound like, that gravity of loneliness and fear and oppressive dread.

And then he was laughing.

It was a sad laugh, maybe even a crazy laugh, and I felt sure it was about some old memory they'd come upon together, like something valuable glistening at the bottom of clear water, and now they were holding it up to the sunlight and turning it around for observation, and enjoying themselves with the beautiful simplicity of children.

When I came back in, she was kneeling next to him and her head was in his lap as if he were her father. His hand looked knuckled and outsize on the slender beauty of her head.

"You go now, Cindy."

"I don't want to leave you."

"Payne's right."

"Payne doesn't give a damn about you. Or me. He wants to keep Chief Gibbs happy."

"Go now. Please."

She glanced up at him and saw that he was not likely to change his mind. Once again, she glowered in my direction, then got slowly to her feet, her khaki uniform wrinkled, her eyes red from crying.

I said, "I'll give you an hour to get back to town and then I'll bring him in."

"You really are a white man, Payne," she sneered. "Only a white man would think I'd care about my career that much."

"He's right," Rhodes said again. "You have to worry about your career."

I held her gun out to her. She couldn't hide her surprise.

"What's this for?"

"You come back to town without your gun, it's going to look damned funny."

"What's to stop me from taking it and shooting you?"

"Nothing."

"You're crazy if you don't think I'd like to."

"But I don't think you will."

She nodded to Rhodes. "He'll never get a fair trial. You should let him run."

"I can't let him run. You know that."

"White people make me sick. Did I ever tell you that?"

Obviously she was insinuating something about last night but didn't want to hurt Rhodes' feelings by making it any plainer. She was doing a good job of hurting my feelings, which was her intent.

"You go on now," Rhodes said, sounding more tired than before. "He'll take care of me all right."

Another glare at me.

She walked over and kissed him. It was almost maternal, that kiss. The way she slid her arm around his shoulder, she was a mountain lioness defending her cub from all peril. You'd be crazy to go up against her at this moment unless you absolutely had to.

Then she was done and she stood up and walked over to me.

She spat in my face.

All sorts of feelings went through me. I felt more alone at that moment, I think, than at any time since my wife died.

While Rhodes was looking embarrassed for me, she stalked out of the cabin, khaki legs rasping against each other as she moved.

Only then did I realize what had just happened. When she'd gone over to kiss him, she'd slipped him her service revolver.

He had the .38 Smith & Wesson in his right hand and he was just bringing it up to the level of my chest.

And I was starting to bring my Ruger up, too.

Right here, in this small cabin, we were going to shoot it out.

And then he did something I never would have expected.

Another snapshot: Rhodes turning the gun around, putting the long barrel of it in his open mouth. Me, just now understanding what he was going to do, starting to lunge forward at him, trying to stop him but—

Too late.

He got a good clean barking shot off, one that carried maybe half the back of his head away and affixed it, with blood and hair and shimmering pieces of brain meat, to the rough wall behind him.

She came screaming in, terrified of what she was going to find.

She didn't seem to see me at all, went right past me, right up to him, and dropped to her knees again, and held him, mother and child, as his eyes rolled back dead white and all force and spirit rushed from his body.

The strange thing was, she didn't cry at all, just rocked him gently back and forth, back and forth, easing his soul across the great dark river, to the other side where sweet warm eternity awaits all us sad and frightened mortals.

3

ONE

In the fall, a librarian sent me a Xerox copy of a pioneer wife's journal. Not all the pages were there, and not all the handwriting was legible, but I'd been trying to write a piece about pioneers at harvest so this was very helpful.

Among other things, the journal reported how the woman had made mattresses from large quantities of moss stripped from trees; and spun yarn from the hair of wolves and coyotes, material that didn't always work so well; and turned worn canvas from tents and wagon-covers into overcoats; and battled the headcolds and flu of the colder months by rubbing the children with warm goose grease and turpentine.

On the last day of the month, when the fiery leaves of the hills looked like the undulating wings of a vast butterfly, I knelt by the simple stone grave-marker of Katherine Louise Payne in the little country cemetery where I'd buried her. I formed soft words that were something like prayers, and shaped sentimental thoughts that were something like songs, and thought of how long I'd loved her—all the way back to First Communion in 1957—and how long I would love her still, which was for ever.

One day a package came from my friend in the Bureau who'd been checking up on murders involving the mutilation of noses.

The note attached read:

Similar Cases:

Cleveland, November 6, 1978
Syracuse, February 3, 1981
Los Angeles, June 4, 1986
Chicago, June 28, 1989

Robert, these were the cases I found in the computer. When you called originally, I mentioned the possibility of copycat killings. The Syracuse and Los Angeles murders received national attention.

Best,
RD

I spent a lot of time around the story-and-a-half colonial farm-house my wife had picked out for us, putting a new roof on the garage; making cider from bright red apples the neighbors had dropped by; taking the cats Tasha, Crystal and Tess in for their annual checkups; flying the old biplane every chance

I got; and talking to a university publisher in Ames about possibly submitting my book of Iowa history when I was a little further along with it.

At dusk, I usually went for walks, the frost just starting to silver the pumpkin patches and the forlorn scarecrow on the horizon and the thin disc of cloudy moon riding the prairie night.

At home, I warmed up some cider in the microwave and sat with the cats in the library watching movies of the thirties and forties on American Movie Classics. I'd developed this rather boyish crush on Jean Arthur and watched everything she was in. I tried not to think about how much she reminded me of Kathy.

There was enough money in the savings account so that I didn't have to take any jobs for a while. And then the month was suddenly October, and the cats had taken to wanting the winter blankets out on the bed they let me share with them.

"Payne?"

"Yes."

"Richard Gibbs here."

"Hi, Chief."

Chief Gibbs and I weren't enemies but we weren't friends, either, so anything he called me with was not going to be good news.

"How you doing?" he said.

"Chief?"

"Yeah?"

"Did something happen to Cindy?"

"She quit. Or tried to."

"Her job, you mean?"

"Right. I finally convinced her to just take an extended leave."

"What happened?"

"She decided to do a little investigating on her own."

"I guess I don't understand."

Pause. "She doesn't think that David Rhodes killed those two women."

"Why else would he have committed suicide if he hadn't?"

"That's what I told her."

"Where is she now?"

"That's the trouble." He was a man who spoke in circles. He went on: "She took a little room for herself in Cedar Rapids and that's where she's staying."

"Why Cedar Rapids?"

"Because she's convinced that Perry Heston killed those two women."

"Why Heston?"

"She's got some cockeyed theory. You'd have to ask her." Pause. "And that's why I'm calling you. So you can ask her personally what she's up to."

"You have her address in Cedar Rapids?"

"Yeah, I do, but that's not where you'll find her right at the moment."

"Where would I find her right at the moment?"

"You know the county jail over on May's Island?"

"Sure."

"That's where she is right now."

"What the hell's she doing there?"

"Heston, who is one powerful sumbitch locally let me tell you, had her arrested last night for criminal trespass."

"What was she doing?"

"He has this house out on a lake, this private deal where he and his pals go if you get my drift, and she was peeking in the windows."

"God."

Pause. "She hasn't been quite right in the head since David turned that gun on himself."

"You think Rhodes killed those women, don't you?"

"Hell, yes, I do. He killed them because he saw them as evil. They were madames, in essence, and they dealt Indian girls and David went over to their place a lot of nights and chased away the johns and even roughed up the two women."

"You're sure of this?"

"I looked into things all good and proper after David committed suicide. Cindy wouldn't let me rest until I'd come up with a real plausible story for David killing himself. So I checked things out—with the help of the Cedar Rapids cops— and that's what we came up with. David was an alcoholic with a violent temper and he didn't like seeing teenage girls, especially teenage Indian girls, getting put on the market by a couple of old whores.''

"That still doesn't explain why he killed himself.''

"Now you sound like her.'' Sigh. "He did it because he didn't want to go to prison. That's not so hard to understand.''

"How much is her bail?''

"I really appreciate this. It's a thousand dollars.''

"Steep.''

"Told you, Heston's got clout.''

"You know she hates me.''

"I'm aware of that.''

"Maybe she won't let me bail her out.''

"Hard to imagine somebody turning down a free pass out of jail.''

"The hell of it is,'' I said, "I care about her.''

"I know you do and so do I, and that's why I thought I'd give you a call.''

"You don't see any way possible that Heston would have killed those two women?''

"For what? Maybe they supplied him with a few hookers here and there. He'd kill them for that? Don't make a whole hell of a lot of sense when you think about it.''

"I guess it doesn't.''

"Tell her we're all thinking about her.''

"I will.''

"And tell her she's welcome back, as long as she doesn't get into any more trouble. I mean, the criminal trespass she can probably get dropped, if she has any kind of lawyer at all, but anything stiffer than that . . . well, I can't have my people getting into situations like that.''

"I'll tell her.''

"And tell her I miss her, too. She's a damned good cop

and a lot more fun to be around than the rest of my force, believe me.''

I smiled. "Why don't I just tell her that you think she's a whole lot prettier than your nephew?''

"Yeah. She'd like that. Yeah, tell her that.''

I said goodbye.

Five minutes later, I left for Cedar Rapids.

TWO

The Linn County jail sits on May's Island where, the story goes, lived one of the town's very first citizens, way back in the 1840s. It was also said that he was a horse-thief, and ultimately hanged in Missouri for his predilection. I find none of that especially difficult to believe. While many pioneers were. sound fine people, some were fugitives whose illicit hearts were not transmuted in the beauty and heat of the prairies.

The jail is just a few years old, overlooks the Cedar River on three sides, and has virtually no parking spaces. There's no room. This end of the island is overwhelmed by the venerable Linn County courthouse, which takes up most of the space.

The jail woman was brisk, efficient and far more friendly than I might have expected.

She explained that the bail had to be cash only, that the sum was $1,000, and that 100 per cent had to be paid before the prisoner would be set free. I gave her ten crisp $100 bills, she counted them out and then pointed to the waiting area where a sad-eyed woman with three very noisy children stared wearily out the window. I doubted that this was the first time she had stared out this window with the same eternal beaten gaze.

A uniformed jailer opened the door at the far end of the waiting area. Cindy came out fast. She didn't even look at me. Her eyes homed in on the front door. She was a heat-seeking missile, sensing her target.

I didn't really fall into step with her until we reached the parking area. The day smelled of river and autumn and morning sunlight.

"Don't expect me to say thank you."

"Fair enough," I said.

"I'll pay you back right away."

"No hurry."

She started gazing around for my car. The only one she'd seen was the rental. I had a green Saab. She didn't know that yet.

She was lovely as ever, all cheekbones and girlish freckles and quick chocolate eyes whose approval you found yourself wanting desperately. She looked tired, and her amber blouse and jeans were wrinkled, but there was wiry strength in her every move.

"I didn't kill him," I said.

"I don't want to talk about it."

I grabbed her and spun her around and gripped her arm. I was angry and hurt and a couple of people were passing by, gawking, and I didn't give a damn at all, not right at this moment.

"I couldn't stop him. I didn't know he was going to kill himself any more than you did."

"You could've knocked the gun from his hand."

"Right, Cindy. And then I could've levitated it right out the door." I grasped her arm harder. "There wasn't time to stop him. I tried to jump at him but it was too late. I did all I could, Cindy. But he wanted to die and he wasn't going to let anybody stop him. Do you understand that?"

My voice must have been pretty loud.

A pair of cops, male-female, were walking from the parking lot to the front of the jail, giving me lingering, suspicious looks. This probably went on here a lot. Man and woman quarreling, right after one or the other of them has been bailed out.

"Which one's your car?"

"The green Saab. You're leaning against it."

We got in the car and drove away.

"Perry Heston killed those two women, not David."

"Why would Heston kill them?"

"They had something on him."

"Like what?"

"I don't know. But he was paying them money."

"How do you know that?"

"Sandy's daughter told me."

"I didn't think Patty Moore liked you very much."

"She doesn't. She thinks I hate being Indian, which isn't true. But anyway, she talked to me."

I drove through Cedar Rapids, taking the river road out to Ellis Park. She told me she had an aunt on the other side of the marina where she was staying.

The trees gave the sluggish river grace, blooming fires against the hard blue autumn sky, a hawk gliding low along the railroad tracks that ran in the hills on the top of steep limestone cliffs.

"You're not going to let go of it, are you?"

"No," she said quietly, watching the day.

"Why would your husband have killed himself if he hadn't murdered those women?"

"He did it for some other reason—something he was ashamed of."

"Murder isn't something to be ashamed of?"

She shook her fine sleek silken hair. I wanted to feel the back of her head nestle into the palm of my hand, the way it had so many long nights ago now.

"He wasn't ashamed of murder because he didn't commit murder, Payne. He really didn't. There's the driveway."

A small white clapboard house in need of paint and a new chimney sat on the edge of a grassy hill overlooking a bend in the river. It was peaceful up here and people with homes that had cost twenty times as much didn't have a view half as good. The nearest neighbor was probably a quarter-mile away and yet the house was still within city limits. Perfect.

I turned in the seat. "You get in any more trouble, Gibbs'll have to fire you."

She faced me, too. "I know. But I don't have any choice."

"Before I went to the jail, I made up my mind."

"About what?"

"I'm going to give you an early Christmas present."

"What?"

"Three days of my time. Free gratis."

She teared up. Put her head down. Started crying softly. "All I can think of was when I spat in your face."

"Yeah, I guess I think about that sometimes, too."

"I'm really not like that, Payne, I'm really not. That day I was so worried about David, I was crazy. Literally nuts, I think."

"I know."

"I'm so sorry."

She reached out and took my hand and raised it to her perfect cheek which was warm and wet with her tears.

"I shouldn't let you help me."

"I want to help you. I volunteered to help you. I want you to keep your job. You worked too damned hard to lose it now." I paused. "And that's what David wanted too, you keeping your job. I didn't give much of a damn for him but I did see a different side of him in the cabin that day. He didn't love you but he cared about you and he wanted the best for you. And for him, that meant keeping your job."

She lowered my hand from her cheek to her knee. The warmth of her flesh just below the surface of denim was far more exciting than I wanted it to be right now.

"What are you going to do?"

"I'm not sure," I said. "But I'll keep you informed." I hesitated. "But I've got to be honest."

"You think David killed them?"

"Right."

"And you think that at the end of three days, that's still what you're going to find?"

"Yes."

She leaned over and kissed me tenderly on the mouth.

"Then I appreciate what you're doing all the more. I really do."

"You just take it easy," I said. "Rest and relax. Walk the hills around here."

She looked out at the day again. For the first time since leaving the jail, I saw a modest smile on her most appealing mouth. "God, that is what I should do, isn't it? Walk back in those hills . . . Maybe if I walk at dusk, I'll see a hawk moon."

"What's that?"

"My people believe that when you see a hawk fly across the face of the moon you'll have good luck for many moons to come."

"Then I hope you have a hawk moon."

She held my hand a long moment and it felt wonderful. "The same for you, Robert. A hawk moon for you, too."

I drove back to town.

Thirty-five minutes later, I pulled up in the parking lot behind the three two-story buildings that made up Heston-Cook Computers, Inc.

Inside, I took an elevator to the second floor and stepped off the car into a nicely appointed reception area. Muted blues and grays played off cherrywood wainscotting. Lawyers

would envy the office and the receptionist. Intelligent,
friendly and very definitely female and every bit as muted as
the décor. Behind her, a trim gray-haired lady searched a
three-drawer file cabinet for some papers.

"I'd like to see Mr. Heston," I said.

"I'm afraid he's not here."

"Then Mr. Cook will do fine."

"I'm afraid he's not here, either."

"I see. Will they be back later today?"

"I'm afraid they're away on business."

I wasn't sure why but I was sure she was hiding something.
For just the tiniest moment her azure-colored eyes had evaded
mine as she spoke.

"Then they'll be back tomorrow?"

"I believe so, yes."

"I see."

"Do you have a card?"

"Sure." I gave her my card.

Something died in her face and voice. "Private investiga-
tions," she read aloud.

"And psychological profiling. That's my main occupation."

"Oh."

I had the feeling that the moment I left she was going to
throw my card away and wash her hands in hot soapy water.

"You'll tell them I was here?"

"Of course."

"I appreciate it."

I was just turning to walk back to the elevator when I was
joined by the trim blue-suited gray-haired woman who'd been
searching the filing cabinet. She was one of those sixty-year-
olds who manage to stay cute as hell.

We boarded the elevator. The doors closed.

She said, "I heard what you asked Maureen. About Mr.
Heston and Mr. Cook. I guess I don't blame her for not telling
you."

"For not telling me what?"

She sighed. "I've never heard anything like it."

The elevator reached the first floor and the doors opened. I held the door at bay and said, "Heard anything like what?"

"Their argument. They were in Mr. Heston's office shouting and swearing at each other and smashing things. And then they both left very quickly. Nobody's seen them for two days."

"Left together?"

"Yes. After Mr. Heston got a phone call."

I smiled. "I should pay you to spy for me."

She didn't smile in return. "I just thought maybe you could help them in some way. I have this terrible feeling that something is very, very wrong."

"Morning, Martha," said a sturdy no-nonsense man whose bulk shook the car when he boarded it. He pretended I didn't exist. He punched the button. He was in a hurry and the world would just have to get used to it.

I nodded goodbye to her through the closing doors.

―――――

There was a belief among many white people that red men would kill them at virtually any opportunity. For this reason, prisons often kept red men isolated from white. Indians generally received poorer food and poorer medical attention. Over 30% of Indians died during prison stays of more than six years.
                    Professor David Cromwell's Indian Journal

November 1, 1903

Anna continued to investigate Gray House, her enquiries, discreet as she could make them, leading her to a man named Rudolph Hvacek who had been Douglas Ashlock's first employee.

He now worked for another wealthy family in town as a gardener.

"I really don't see why you need to talk to me."

"I just have a few questions, Mr. Hvacek."

"Are these official questions?"

"I'm not sure what you mean."

"Did the Chief send you here?"

"Well . . ."

"I didn't think so. I don't like being questioned by a female police officer in the first place—a lot of people in this town aren't happy that you're wearing that badge, Miss Tolan— and I particularly don't like being questioned when the Chief doesn't even know you're here."

Mr. Hvacek had a nice little apartment for himself out on the 800 block of First Avenue West. He was fortyish, plump, and fitted into a black suit that an undertaker would envy. Like many servants, he had begun to think of himself as a member of the upper classes. His contempt for Anna was pretty easy to see.

"It's about the Indian girl who was killed here last spring," Anna told him, "after Douglas Ashlock moved his family into town and started using Gray House for his fun. I believe the group was called 'The Circle of Six.' That Indian girl was there all the time, wasn't she?"

They were in the parlor of the apartment house. Hvacek sat up primly. "I don't believe you understand. I'm not going to answer any more of your questions."

"I've checked my facts Mr. Hvacek. You continued to work for Mr. Ashlock even after Gray House was officially closed down, so you know everything that went on there. You know about the Indian girl."

"That is quite enough, Miss Tolan. Quite enough."

Without another word, he escorted her to the door and out into the bracing night air.

"Hi, Anna."

"Hi, Trace."

"May I come up and sit on the porch with you?"

"If you like."

"Wow. It's baking out tonight."

"It sure is."

"I suppose you want to know about my date with Marietta Evans last night?"

"Not really, Trace."

"Well, we had a darned good time."

"Good."

"What'd you do?"

"Last night?"

"Uh-huh."

"Played bridge with Mrs. Goldman and her friends."

"That sounds like fun."

"Are you being sarcastic?"

"No."

"Good. Because I like bridge and I like Mrs. Goldman and her friends."

"People said we made a very handsome couple."

"You and Marietta?"

"Uh-huh."

"Good."

"She's very pretty."

"Yes, she is."

"God, Anna, don't you know what I'm trying to do?"

"Sure, you idiot. You're trying to make me jealous and I'm trying to pretend not to *be* jealous."

"Actually, she has kind of an overbite and bad breath."

"You got close enough to smell her breath?"

"I didn't kiss her, if that's what you mean."

"Really?"

"C'mon, Anna, you know better than that. I just figured I'd make you jealous and you'd be so happy to see me that you'd—"

"I'd what?"

"You know."

"No, I don't know."

"Gosh, Anna, won't you just marry me, won't you please?"

"I'm not sure I want to, Trace. I mean, a part of me does, but—"

Soon after, Trace, his head low, left the porch and walked down the shadowy street until Anna could no longer see him.

THREE

I peered through a screen door into an orderly apartment of recently waxed hardwood floors and very neatly arranged furniture. From a distant room came the sounds of an acoustic guitar playing something that sounded vaguely Spanish, and much nearer by was the smell of sweet furniture polish.

I knocked.

She came out less than a minute later and at first I didn't recognize her at all. The dark hair had been cut, for one thing, in a plucky boyish bob. And the chambray shirt and tan chinos showed off a slender body she'd previously buried beneath several layers of clothing.

This was Sandy Moore's daughter. Slightly less than five weeks ago her apartment had been a rat's nest of trash and grime. So had she. Only the dark sparkling eyes were recognizable.

"Hi."

"Hi, Patty."

She giggled. "I don't mind if you stare."

"God, what happened?"

"C'mon in and I'll tell you."

I went in. She got me a Diet Pepsi from the refrigerator, carried it to where I sat in a faded but spotless armchair, and then sat crosslegged on the newly waxed floor and said, "That night you were here asking me all those questions about my mom and David Rhodes?"

"Right."

"I went nuts. After you left, I mean. Started hitting bars and everything. Woke up in this guy's place—hadn't ever seen him before—and tried to kill him."

"Why?"

She shrugged. "Just because I was so sick of it all—of being me, I mean. You know, being a slave to the bottle and all." She laughed merrily. "Luckily, he woke up and saw me with the knife there and took it away from me."

"Then what?"

"Then I came home and took pills and turned on the gas and tried to kill myself. But a neighbor smelled it and got me to the Mercy Hospital. After they pumped my stomach, I decided I might as well go detox. They've got a clinic there. I stayed three weeks."

"You're dry?"

"Twenty-seven days' worth."

"Congratulations."

"Yeah. I'm proud of myself, I really am. I'm scared, too, of course. I could fall right back off."

"And speaking of falling off—you're not going to chase after the rodeo, I take it?"

Shook her head. There was an impishness new to the dark eyes. It was fun to see. "Nah. If all those hunky rodeo Indians want somebody of my quality, they can come chase me."

"Good idea."

"How's your Diet Pepsi?"

"Vintage."

A grin. Glance around the living room. "You ever think I could make it look this good?"

"Honest?"

"Honest."

"No. I figured this place was just about to be condemned."

"Got my old job back at the hotel. They're not crazy about Indians but as this black woman who works there says, 'Honey, least they don't hate you as much as they hate us.' " This time there was sorrow in the laughter. I liked her a whole hell of a lot, and admired her, too.

"You're probably here about my mom, huh?"

"Yeah."

"Anything special?"

"I was wondering if you'd let me look through her effects."

"If you want to, I guess."

"I wouldn't take anything. I'd just look, I mean. You could stand right next to me."

"The clothes and stuff I already gave away to St. Vincent de Paul's."

"Any other stuff?"

"Odds and ends in a couple of cardboard boxes. You know what you're looking for?"

"Not exactly."

The grin. "Didn't figure you did." Pause. "You still don't think David Rhodes killed her and my aunt?"

"I do."

"But Cindy doesn't?"

"Yeah. Something like that."

"She always could get pathetic about him. Even when she was a little girl, my mom said."

"She's a nice woman."

Impish glance. "I'll take your word for it. I told you before—she's one of those people who're ashamed of being Indian, I guess, and I never can bring myself to feel too sorry

for them.'' She stood up, graceful as her legs disentangled.
''You want to go see her stuff?''

"Sure.''

We sat in a sunny bedroom on a hook rug, looking through
a cardboard box, the contents of which represented her
mother's life. Patty had scrubbed and waxed up this room,
too, and the double bedspread smelled pleasantly of fabric
softener, and the shafts of sunlight on the bureau brought out
the deep chestnut colors of the old but fine quality wood.

We went to work on the box, the one with the Campbell's
soup can on the side.

It contained programs from several years' worth of Pow-
Wows that the La Costa put on for tourists each summer; red
ribbons and blue ribbons and yellow ribbons and green ribbons; a slender Bulova watch that no longer kept time; a half-
dozen or so inexpensive rings; a well-read paperback of *Love
Story*; a fragile crucifix with the Christ figure broken in half
and glued back together; and photographs of Sandy at various
ages and in various emotional states. Most of the photos
showed her posing in front of rock concerts and other hippie
gatherings. In the background you could see signs advertizing
THE STONES and BOB DYLAN and PINK FLOYD, the mid-
seventies mostly. In these photos, Sandy was thin and pretty
in a beaten way, the quick feral way of a junkie, which I
suspected she'd been.

''She looked so vulnerable.''

''Yes, she did,'' I said.

''I wish we'd have gotten along better.''

I nodded and she took my hand and said, ''Could I just
hold it for a minute?'' She was trying not to cry.

''It's a dollar fifty for every three minutes.''

''Sort of like one of those sex phone hot lines?''

''Something like that, yes.''

She put her head back against the bed. ''Our problem was
we were both addicts and that makes for a pretty shitty relationship.''

''It does indeed.''

"What I said about Cindy in there, about her not being able to deal with being an Indian?"

"Uh-huh."

"I shouldn't have said that. I hate it when I get sanctimonious like that. Somebody hurts you and you want to hurt them back. Cindy's always been a little high-handed with most of us and I guess I've always resented it." She sat up straight again. "I guess being dry doesn't automatically turn you into a nice person, does it?"

"I don't think so."

She smiled. "You want to look some more."

"Great."

We went back to the box.

More photos. A good dozen showed Sandy and Karen Moore with a variety of prosperous-looking white men. I imagined that these dated back to the days when they'd been hookers rather than procuresses. In the seventies they'd both worn a lot of tie-dye stuff as well as platform heels and those outsize poofy black hats favored by black pimps, at least in the black action films of the time.

Patty was the one who turned it up.

"I wonder who that is," she said.

"Who?"

"See in the background, back by the trees."

"Oh. Right. The little girl."

"I've never seen this before. She looks kind of familiar."

"Yes, she does."

"Really? To you, too?"

"Uh-huh. But I don't know why."

"And she's with both of them, Mom and Karen, I mean."

"Is that odd or something?"

"A little bit around the edges, anyway. I mean, Mom would occasionally babysit the neighbors' kids when she was around the apartment—but why would both Mom and Karen have a kid with them?"

"I don't know."

"And you know where I think this was taken?"

"Where?"

"Schaefer Park."

"You know, I think you're right." I stared at the photo some more. Schaefer Park is the one that is left in a reasonably natural state. No zoo. No rides for the kids. No ice-skating rinks. Just a park with a lot of paths angling through deep woods. Gays and junkies use it a lot at night for assignations. But the photo was twenty years old, back when both Schaefer Park and the world were much more innocent.

"Turn it over," I said. "See if there's a date."

She turned it over. No date. No identification of any kind.

"But look at what they're wearing," Patty said.

"Seventies?"

"Definitely."

"Can you get any closer than that?"

"You mean like 1975 or 1978 or something like that?"

"Uh-huh."

"Let me just look at it a minute."

"All right."

"Wow."

"What?"

"I didn't realize what blouse that was at first."

"The one your mom's wearing?"

"Right. I bought it for her with my own money. My first job. I was a cashier out at this discount store and I bought it for her fortieth birthday."

"You're sure that's the blouse?"

"Positive."

"So what year would it have been?"

"Seventy-nine."

I stared at the girl in the photo some more. No older than nine or ten max. Dark pigtails. An Indian girl, obviously. She wore jeans and a white blouse and even in a somewhat fuzzy shot, even from her distant place in the frame, her body language suggested a certain sadness. The brown eyes appealed to a world that neither saw nor listened.

"Your mom ever mention your Aunt Karen keeping a little girl for somebody?"

"No."

"Maybe Karen was babysitting this little girl and they just took her to the park."

"Possible, I suppose."

"But you don't think so?"

"No," she said, "and I don't think you think so, either."

"No, I guess I don't."

She tapped the photo. "You can borrow that if you have copies made."

"I appreciate that."

"But I still think he did it."

"David?"

"Uh-huh."

She walked me to the front door. I was still impressed with what she'd done with herself and her apartment.

"You keep me posted?" she said.

"Sure."

"I hope you can find out who that little girl is." Then she looked at me. "You already know, don't you, Robert?"

"Pardon me?"

"You know who she is. A couple of minutes ago, I was watching your face when you looked at the photo and I saw your expression. I think you know who she is."

"You should be a detective."

"You going to tell me about her?"

"Not right now. Later, when I'm sure."

She indicated the photo. "I think maybe I know who she is, too." She smiled. "Thanks for letting me hold your hand."

"My pleasure."

Her smile was warm, teasing. "So how much do I owe you?"

"Huh?"

"You said you charged a dollar fifty for every three minutes. To hold your hand."

"Today was a free introductory offer."

"I appreciate that."

I took her hand again. "The pleasure's all mine, believe me."

I found a place that would make six black-and-white copies of the photo by the end of the working day. Then I drove ·out First Avenue to the new apartment house I'd visited.

I parked a quarter-block from the front of the place and prepared myself for a long wait. There was always the possibility that she wasn't home. That would make for an even longer wait.

FOUR

One hour and twenty-three minutes later, she emerged from the driveway in a silver Neon. She wore dark glasses, a red button-down shirt and looked fetching as always.

She turned right and I followed her.

The mall on this end of town was crowded with cars in from surrounding towns. On weekends the farmers arrive and the merchants are happy to see them. They come to buy, not gawk. Nobody would drive this far to gawk.

She parked her Neon up by Younkers and quickly vanished inside.

I did some more waiting. I could have followed her inside but there was always the chance that I'd lose her and she'd get away.

I spent most of the time leaning against my car and looking out at all the construction going on up and down Collins Road. The urban planners have decided that the north-east quadrant is the next major development area, and the chains are making all this come true. I once heard a somewhat paranoid theory that most urban planners are actually on the take from real-estate tycoons. The tycoons tell the planners which land to sell, and the planners then announce the site of the next boom. Self-fulfilling prophecy. The proud originator of this theory was Gilhooley, Cedar Rapids' only resident Maoist, so I don't necessarily take it seriously.

She came out one hour and four big packages later.

She must have been caught up in her thoughts because she didn't see me until I opened her car door for her and took the first paper-rattling package from her hand.

"I could always call a policeman."

"Yes, you could," I said. "But then I'd have to tell them how man Heston and Cook are paying you to be their mistress, and Heston and Cook would get awfully upset."

"What you said isn't true."

"Right."

"Goddamn you, what do you want anyway?"

"Coffee."

"What?"

"I want you to have some coffee with me."

"You bastard."

There was a Denny's not far away and we sat next to a big window and watched the summer die. There was a real melancholy about it all now, the old folks in their bright merry summer clothes that looked wrong with the leaves turning, and the teenagers who'd just entered senior year loud with lust and hope and bone-deep terror about the world of adulthood awaiting them.

"Perry is going to be very, very pissed when I tell him about this."

"Is he now?"

"Apparently you aren't sure how important he is."

"If I didn't know, I'm sure he'd tell me."

She still had the dark glasses on.

I slid a dollar across the Formica table to her.

"What's this?"

"It's yours if you'll take those glasses off."

"Very funny."

"I want to show you something."

"I don't want to see it."

"And I want you to look at it with your glasses off."

"You seem to be under the impression that you have the fucking right to give me fucking orders."

"Would you like more coffee?" the waitress said, trying heroically to pretend that she hadn't heard the line that Linda Prine had just snapped at me.

"Yes, please," I said. "Darling, how about you?"

She didn't say anything.

"My wife has a sore throat. Resting her voice. She'll have another black coffee, too."

The waitress nodded, glancing once at Darling in her dark glasses, then went away.

"Very funny. Well—What is it you want to show me? I'll look at it and then I want you to drive me back to my car and then I'm going to tell Perry and you're going to be in very, very big trouble. Very big."

"You're taking your glasses off?"

She fairly tore them off.

She glared at me out of that sad but sexy waif face of hers, angel of the alley.

I took the photo from my pocket and put it down on the table between us.

She visibly started.

"That's you, isn't it, the little girl?"

Her voice had changed. The anger was gone. She sounded weary suddenly. "Where did you get this?"

"Sandra Moore's daughter gave it to me."

"That's what I figured."

"How long did you know Karen and Sandy?"

She raised her head slowly. Tears shone in her eyes. "Would you please take me back to my car?"

The waitress was back. The last time my Darling wife had been using the f-word. This time she was crying. We must have looked like an awfully happy couple.

I took a five out and dropped it on the table. "That's for you."

"Thanks," the waitress said.

In the car, her glasses back on, Linda Prine said, "You have no right to do any of this."

"I'm not sure anymore that David Rhodes killed those two women."

"Then who did?"

"Perry or Bryce, maybe."

"Or me?"

"Possibly."

"Why would Perry or Bryce kill them?"

"They were paying both women blackmail."

"I really don't want to talk about this anymore."

And she didn't.

She got out of my car and into hers without a word.

"You find out anything more about that Circle of Six, Gilhooley?"

"Yeah, I did, matter of fact. I mean, nothing anybody could ever prove. But, man, it is really kinky. Remember that old newspaper guy I told you about? The one who published the Labor paper?"

"I remember you mentioning him."

"What he told me, man. Heavy duty . . . real heavy duty." He sounded exultant. A scandal involving the city's élite was bound to make a Maoist happy.

"Where'll you be?" I asked.

"You remember Fred's place?"

"That pool hall?"

"Yeah. I'm playing pool with this woman in about two hours. She was watching me the other day and said she'd play me for five bucks. I wasn't having a good day the other day so she got all wired up about beating me because I'm supposed to be good and everything. But she had to leave before I could get to her so today's the big day.''

"You're a good shooter, Gilhooley.''

"Yeah, and this woman's about to find out how good. Plus she's a lawyer and you know how I hate lawyers.''

"Yeah, lawyers and bus drivers.''

"Damn straight.''

"And mailmen.''

"And don't forget advertizing people.''

"Oh, right,'' I said, "advertizing people.'' His second wife—he'd had three thus far—was in advertizing so he tended to blame her occupation for their terrible relationship. Not the fact that he was a) something of a nag b) something of a hothead and c) something of a crazy man. No, it had been the fault of her occupation. He invariably referred to ad people with that great sneering rage only a true Maoist can summon, as "showbiz wannabes''—for him a completely devastating judgement. What good Maoist ever wanted to be in showbiz?

"Anyway, I'll be there the next couple of hours. I'm going to cream this chick, believe me.''

"I'll see you in a while, then.''

"Wait till you hear this, man. This is a really wild story, what these six guys did back then.''

While some condemned white men occasionally peti-
tioned the courts for new trials and so forth, red men
and black men were generally denied further access to
lawyers. Their execution dates came swiftly and without
any legal hesitation.
                    Professor David Cromwell's Indian Journal

November 2, 1903

"I believe you know this gentleman, Anna,'' Chief Ryan said to Anna the next morning.

Anna nodded. "Yes, of course. It's Mr. Ashlock.''

Ashlock was an imposing man, handsome in a way that

combined the spirit of the rake with the conniving air of a lawyer. He wore a dark business suit and conservative blue cravat and white shirt. He looked tired and unhappy.

"Mr. Ashlock would like to say something to you, Anna."

"All right."

Ashlock had seated himself on the edge of the Chief's desk. His importance seemed to fill the entire office. He said, "I understand you've been investigating me, Anna."

"Yes, sir, I have."

"Would you care to tell me why?"

"Because I believe that Tall Tree is innocent and that you murdered the Indian girl."

"Anna!" Chief Ryan said.

But Ashlock said, "Let her speak, Chief."

"I have certain evidence."

"You do, eh?"

"Yes, Mr. Ashlock, I do."

"Would you care to tell me about that evidence?"

"If the Chief gives me permission."

Ashlock didn't even look at the Chief. He simply said, "I'm giving you permission, and that's enough."

She glanced at the Chief. He nodded.

"Very well, sir," Anna said. And then told him what she'd found.

"This 'scientific detection' of yours, it sounds very clever."

"Thank you, sir."

"Unfortunately, it doesn't have a damn thing to do with the truth."

Anna said nothing.

Ashlock stood up, walked over to her, his boots loud on the wooden floor. He looked down into her eyes and said, "I didn't kill her, Anna."

"All right, sir."

"And I expect your investigation to end now that I've officially denied your suspicions. Is that correct?"

But the Chief didn't give Anna a chance to answer. He got up from behind his desk and came around to join them. "Of course her investigation will end. And right now. You can bet I'll see to it, Mr. Ashlock, and see to it right away.''

Ashlock picked up his bowler, his icy blue eyes never once leaving Anna's face.

"It was very nice meeting you, Officer Tolan."

"Nice meeting you, sir."

He nodded to the Chief and left.

Anna felt more certain than ever that he was the killer.

The Chief said, "Now, Anna, I want you to tell me just what the hell you've been up to."

She had never seen him more upset than he was at this moment.

"I need to tell you something, Anna."

"I know. You're going to have another date with Marietta."

"No. Something else."

She had never heard him sound like this. Or look like this. "What is it?"

"When I went east last month?"

"Uh-huh." She knew this was going to be terrible. Her whole body ached in anticipation.

"I met an old high-school classmate of mine. Jenna Thompson. She came back to Cedar Rapids right after I did and—well, we've kind of been seeing each other."

"I see."

"And things kind of developed real fast."

"I understand."

"And we're—well, we're engaged."

"Oh."

"I'm sorry, Anna."

"So am I, Trace. And a lot of it's my fault. The way I've treated you sometimes. I'm sorry."

For the very first time in over a year, Trace took his leave without even trying to kiss her. He just got up from the porch swing and left.

Anna spent most of the night on her bed. Sometimes she wept. Sometimes she slept.

Mrs. Goldman came in from time to time and sat next to her in the darkness and held her hand and just let her cry until she couldn't cry anymore.

FIVE

The really beautiful houses in Cedar Rapids, at least to me, are still to be found in the areas of Grande and Blake. A few of them date back to the time in the early century when one went spooning on the Cedar in rowboats, and sat on the lawns of Bever Park and listened to barbershop quartets, and watched 4th of July fireworks only after hearing stirring patriotic speeches from one of the New York troupes that regularly played Greene's Opera House. This is old money, and while it has all the faults of old money—arrogance, smugness, and the belief that destiny rather than luck gave the old rich their money in the first place—there is real elegance to be found in these homes and streets, reminding me of F. Scott Fitzgerald's descriptions of St. Paul in the late last century, and how he'd ride his bike past the houses of the rich, and glimpse teenage girls of impossible beauty and poise on the rolling green lawns . . . scenes he would later reproduce in *Gatsby*.

The new rich tend to live in housing developments on the eastern outskirts of the town. True, these are very special housing developments, with half-million-dollar homes and imposing areas of wilderness nearby and security of every sort you can afford. Yet they're still housing developments— eight, ten, twelve large homes corralled into several acres that have been gnawed out of timberland, with plenty of wide streets to accommodate all the BMWs and Porsches and lumbering family vans.

Cedar Rapids is a small but successful city and always has been. Much as we like to complain about generations of hack politicians, the city fathers past (and present) obviously had a pretty good sense of what they were about, especially when you consider that we not only survived the eighties—factory closings, farm foreclosures, the first sad, ragged appearance of homeless people—but are today one of the country's largest exporters *per capita*. Even though I live forty miles outside the city, in a small town and a small town that has aspirations to be nothing more than it is, I still think of myself as a Cedar Rapidian.

All these things were on my mind as I pulled past the open gates leading to a PRIVATE lane of six massive redbrick houses, each furiously designed to look different from the others.

Evelyn Cook, in white halter and red shorts despite the definite autumnal chill on the air, was watering her front yard. She watched me drive up and park, but as soon as I got out of the car she turned back to her watering.

The closer I got, the better she looked in her simple appealing sexuality, the body that should have long ago slid into fat but hadn't. The velvet push of breasts from the top of her halter; the shining blonde down on her firm white thighs; the merry hint of lust in the cornflower-blue eyes. Usually, anyway. Today there was no hint of merriment at all.

"Hi, remember me?"

She kept on watering her lawn. "Of course."

"Wondered if your husband was around?"

Shook her blonde head. "He's at work."

"That's funny."

"What is?" She still hadn't looked at me. Apparently found her lawn one hell of a lot more fascinating than she found me.

You got a nice sense of country out here, anyway, I thought, glancing up at the sky to see a hawk sliding down the air currents, and a scarecrow silhouette on the horizon of a distant cornfield.

"What's funny is that at work they told me he hadn't been in for a few days and that he was home sick."

"Oh." She finally looked at me with her sweet little face. "I guess I don't know where he is."

"Just no idea at all, huh?"

"I don't care if you believe me or not."

"Well, you have to admit that it's kind of strange."

"What is?"

"A wife who doesn't know where her husband's been for two days."

"I didn't say two days."

"I see."

"I didn't say two days at all."

She was so sumptuous in the halter and shorts, too bad the sorrow in her eyes sapped her of all vitality. Dark crescents had formed under her blue, blue eyes.

"Then when was the last time you saw him?"

"I didn't see him. But I heard from him."

"When?"

"Last night."

"About what time?"

"I don't have to answer any of these questions, you know."

"I know."

She walked away from me then, her white feet covered with blades and flecks of newly mown grass, walking back and forth several times to finish off her watering.

After a few minutes, she came back to me and shut off the hose. "He called about nine o'clock last night."

"Did he say where he was?"

"No."

"You look scared."

"I am scared."

"He give you any idea of what was going on?"

Shook her head. "He was pretty drunk and he just kept saying, 'It's all gonna come down on me, babe. It's all gonna come down on me.' "

"Do you know what he meant?"

Shook her head again. "No. And I'm not sure I *want* to know."

"Mommy."

A slight but pretty girl of perhaps eight stood on the front porch of the recessed entryway in the front of the large Italian Renaissance house. "Mom, Derek won't give me the blue crayon. He says he doesn't have to because it's his birthday."

"Tell him that even though it's his birthday, he has to give you the blue crayon."

"And the red one?"

"Yes, the red one, too."

"Even the yellow one?"

"Yes, honey, even the yellow one. He has to share all of them with you."

"Thanks, Mommy." The little girl went back inside.

"She's very cute."

"Thanks."

I took the photo from my jacket. "Here's another little girl I want you to see. Does she look familiar at all?"

She took the photo. "No. Should she?"

"I think she has something to do with your husband's trouble."

"A little girl?"

"She's not a little girl anymore. She's twenty-five now."

She handed me back the photo. "He really is in trouble, isn't he. Is it some sort of scandal or something?"

"I'm afraid so."

"What's going to happen?"

"No idea, I'm afraid. Not yet."

I put my hand on her shoulder. The flesh gave me a start, so tender and warm and female. The gesture had been intended merely as courtesy. Or so I'd told myself anyway.

She seemed to read my thoughts, looked at my hand on her shoulder, then back at me. I took my hand away.

"Were you really in the FBI?"

"Yes."

"Good."

"Good?"

"Yes. Then you're not just some sleazy private investigator."

"I do have a license for that."

"You know what I mean."

"I know what you mean."

"Your hand feels nice there." For the first time, she looked older, a certain harshness tightening the blue eyes and the soft erotic mouth. "I'd like to tell Bryce some of the things I was thinking about when you put your hand on my shoulder just now. Not that he'd give a damn." She raised her head and looked up at the sky as if God had written a sentence or two of wisdom for her to read. "Not that he's given a damn in a long time. Not about me, anyway. About the kids, yes. But me . . ."

She shook her head. "Anyway, it felt good. Your hand on my shoulder."

"Felt good to me, too." Then, "Have you talked to Claire Heston today?"

"Yes. Why?"

"How about Perry?"

"I'm not following you."

"Is he missing, too?"

"Sure. They're in it together, whatever it is. So are some of the other boys—all the 'stars' as they like to think of themselves. The thing is, Bryce and Perry are the ones with the most to lose. The most money, the most prestige."

"You really don't have any idea what's going on?"

"Not really."

"Mommy."

This time it was a little boy on the front steps, Derek, presumably. He looked to be a few years younger than his sister. He wore a short-sleeved white shirt and blue trousers and a festive red bow tie. Remnants of a birthday party, no doubt.

"Yes, honey?"

"Stacy says I have to share the crayons with her."

"That's right, honey, you do."

"But it's my birthday."

"Even on your birthday, honey."

"That's not fair, Mommy. What're birthdays for, anyway?"

She glanced at me and smiled with a maternal admixture of pride and exasperation.

"Maybe I'd better go inside."

"I appreciate your time. I'd like to give you my answering service number."

"I'll be glad to take it."

"If I can help . . ."

Sad smile. "I think I'm beyond help right now, Mr. Payne. And so is my husband, I'm afraid."

She went inside.

SIX

Gilhooley smiled and said, "This won't take long."

She was an unlikely-looking pool hustler. She came through the door tall and imposing in a gray pin-striped business suit, carrying an expensive leather briefcase in her right hand and a disassembled pool cue in her left. She had short red hair that framed her freckled pretty face perfectly, and a grin almost as merry as her green eyes.

"You want to break or you want me to?" she said, after telling us her name was Kristin.

"You're a lawyer, huh?" Gilhooley said.

She smiled. "Yeah, they told me you hated lawyers."

"And bus drivers," I said.

"And mailmen," Gilhooley said.

"And advertizing people," I said.

"And veterinarians," Gilhooley said.

"Veterinarians?" I said. "When did that start?"

"I put 'em on the list last week. I'll tell you about it sometime."

"I've never met anybody who hated whole categories of people like that," Kristin said. "That's really weird."

Then she put her cue together and got down to business. She took two twenties from a tiny pocket in her suit jacket and laid them on the edge of the table.

It was right then, I think, that Gilhooley sensed that he'd profoundly underestimated sweet-looking Kristin here. She'd be great in court, with that disarmingly guileless face and those innocently merry eyes.

Forty dollars she'd put down.

Gilhooley looked at the two twenties then at me. "Could you loan me twenty?"

I should have figured that. I've probably loaned Gilhooley somewhere in the vicinity of a thousand dollars over the past four years, ten and twenty at a time, and always within the confines of an ancient smoky pool-hall like this one—you know, where the biker gangs sit around deciding which civilian to give a little grief to. None of them were around this afternoon. They must have gone over to the car wash and walked through the wash part. I hear they do that once a month whether they need to or not.

"So—do you want to break?" Kristin said. "Or shall I?"

"Ladies first."

I think that was the wrong thing to say. For one thing, inherent in it was the kind of patronizing tone that makes most modern women crazy. For another, it probably wasn't a real great idea to piss her off right at the top. The way she'd laid down her two twenties, she seemed to know what she was doing.

"Cute," she said, grinding her teeth and bending over to break the balls.

"There's a consolation prize for losing today," Gilhooley said. "The loser gets to sleep with me."

The merry eyes had never looked merrier. "Then I guess you're going to be sleeping alone as usual, Gilhooley, because I don't intend to lose."

She broke the balls.

She put two spots in different pockets.

"Shit," Gilhooley said.

"Probably beginner's luck," I said.

She then put two more spots in two more different pockets.

"Maybe you shouldn't have said 'Ladies first' Gilhooley," I said.

"Yeah? Just wait till I get my turn," Gilhooley said.

It's sort of painful to watch the male ego crumble that way. So I didn't watch. I walked around the pool-hall. Eight tables, couple Pepsi machines, a john with a mosaic of dirty words on the walls, a wobbly table and chairs that served as a poker set-up, and a radio that was playing one of those totally incomprehensible rap songs that probably had something to do with shooting white guys about my age.

When I got back to the table, Gilhooley said, "You were right. Beginner's luck. I need forty."

"I finally figured out why he hates all those categories of people," Kristin said to me.

"Oh? Why?"

"They probably beat him at pool."

Forlorn as Gilhooley looked, I had to laugh. She was Gilhooley's superior in every respect worth noting.

"Watch me this time," Gilhooley said after I put down two twenties for him. And to Kristin: "Why don't you break again?" He was determined to do his macho-stud routine right up to the end.

"Ladies first?" she said sweetly.

"Yeah," Gilhooley smiled. "Exactly."

This time she didn't even let him have one shot.

He was about to ask me for more money—which I was about to refuse him, my not exactly being independently wealthy—when she checked the watch on her slender shapely wrist and said, "I've got to get back to court. But it was fun."

"If I didn't have this sore throat, I would've been a lot better."

"Well," Kristin said demurely, "I was off my game a little, too. I was abducted by aliens last night and they didn't bring me back until nearly dawn. I just didn't get much sleep."

And then she was gone.

"You know the worst thing?" Gilhooley said, after it was safe to speak again.

"No, what?"

"I think I'm falling in love with her."

Wife number four may just have walked on stage.

A Kiowa Chief once told me that when young Indians were sent off to prison, some among the tribal council pronounced them dead—for even if they did not die physically in prison, they would certainly die spiritually.

Professor David Cromwell's Indian Journal

November 28, 1903

Anna got the deathbed call the night before Hanukkah.

She was downstairs helping Mrs. Goldman collect things to be set out in the parlor—Sabbath candlesticks, Kiddush cup, Hanukkah menorah, Bible, prayer book and several heirlooms—when the telephone bell brayed through the silence.

Anna took the call.

"Anna Tolan?"

"Yes."

"My name is Mrs. Washburn."

"Oh?"

"I'm Mr. Hvacek's landlady."

"Oh. Yes."

"He's dying."

"What happened?"

"He insisted he knew how to ride this horse of my uncle's

and—well, he got thrown. Very bad head injuries. He slips in and out of consciousness. He wants to talk to you."

"Where is he?"

"Mercy Hospital. Room 204."

"I can be there in ten minutes."

"Fine. I'd appreciate it."

Darkened hospital room.

Nuns like great white birds flitting about outside the door.

Hvacek looking old and frail in his deathbed.

"I just want to do right by the Lord, Miss Tolan."

"I understand."

"The young Indian girl."

"Yes?"

"You were right. She was out at Gray House for many years, as soon as Mrs. Ashlock moved into town."

"Many years? You mean she was a little girl when they brought her there?"

"Yes."

A nun came in. "Please, Miss Tolan, you'll have to leave now."

But Hvacek grasped Anna's hand tightly. "Please, Sister, give us one more minute. Alone."

The nun did not look happy but she retreated back to the hallway.

Hvacek looked Anna in the eye. "The girl was going to tell everybody about how she'd been brought there when she was very little and what they did to her. It would've destroyed Ashlock. He *had* to kill her."

And then Hvacek's head lolled to the right and he was unconscious again.

SEVEN

Gilhooley found a place for lunch that served grease not only with its burgers and its fries, but with its fountain Cokes, too. Who says Americans aren't as creative as they used to be?

Over the course of three burgers (two his, one mine; after all, I was paying), Gilhooley told me the following story.

In the 1880s, the streets of working-class London were as filthy and murderous as any outside of Bombay or Calcutta. As with San Francisco's Barbary Coast, policemen tended to travel in packs for their own protection. And there were places where they sometimes simply refused to go. Whitechapel, where Jack the Ripper plied his trade, was one such place. It was one reason he went undiscovered, too. No bobbies wanted to spend time in that part of the East End at night.

The living conditions for the working class were appalling. Fathers and mothers worked for pennies a day at various labors and their children ran completely wild. At night, as many as twenty people slept in the same room—in-laws, family friends, children and adults. There was no sanitation, of course, nor was there anything approaching the Victorian model of proper behavior. Sex, for example, was practiced by people of every age. Indeed, some of the more enterprising parents had taken to selling their children as prostitutes (girls and boys alike) at young ages, and sometimes staged "shows" in alleys for the Victorian gentlemen who enjoyed a night of slumming. One of the great pleasures for these eminent representatives of the upper classes was to watch little children have sex with each other.

As one might imagine, the rate of illegitimate births was astonishing. Girls as young as eleven and twelve bore children. But the infant mortality rate was the great leveler for many of these girls. If the filth of the slums didn't kill the infants, then the girls themselves did. Infanticide was not only condoned, it was frequently encouraged.

Abortion and infanticide were common not only to slum girls but to servant girls as well. The latter were frequently wooed and/or raped by every male member of the upper-class Victorian household. Not only did the master have his way with the girls but so did the son and any friend of father or son. Many of these girls ended up pregnant, of course, and if attempts at abortion failed, they "took a leave" and had their babies at the foundling homes that grew so popular during this era.

While the Victorian age was officially religious, proper and moral, its wealthy and more powerful males indulged in all the license to be found in the reeking shadows of the slums.

You had to understand how these men saw women. Good women, that is to say, their own wives and fiancées, were to reflect and embody all the virtues of the time . . . to be pure, unwise in the ways of sex, "good" in all respects. God help the upper-class woman who did not embody these virtues. We know now that when a husband suspected a wife of being

unfaithful—or even of wanting to be unfaithful—he often
sent her to the family doctor who was instructed to sexually
mutilate the woman so she could no longer enjoy sex. The
doctor, of course, had strong "medical" reasons for this kind
of butchery, and nobody questioned his right to do this, especially since he was acting on the word of the husband.
While this was not what you'd call a frequent practice, it
happened perhaps hundreds of times in that period . . .

The women of the lower classes were another matter entirely.

With these females, upper-class Victorian males felt free to
do anything they desired, however dark or unnatural . . .

This, then, was the London of 1881 when several members
of the House of Lords formed The Circle of Six, a very ex-
clusive club dedicated to debauchery and pleasure.

As we would later learn, it was the purpose of The Circle
of Six to pluck from the vile streets of slum London, girls as
young as five and six. Some were paid for, while others were
simply kidnapped. The six men who made up The Circle
would not touch them at so young an age—for even these
rakes had some moral standards—but they would turn the
girls over to experienced prostitutes who would train them in
the ways of male pleasures . . . so that by the time the girls
were twelve or thirteen, they would know every sexual trick
a man could possibly desire. It was then they were taken to
a lavish manor house outside London to which The Circle
would repair for pleasure . . .

In 1893, a group of midwestern businessmen, among them
two men from Cedar Rapids, visited London and read of The
Circle being exposed by London police. The Royal Family
had fought bitterly against revealing the story—one of the
young girls had died while practicing a most bizarre sex act—
but the police had insisted on prosecution.

And so the six Lords and their Circle became known
through the penny newspapers that feasted on the facts, and
all the lurid speculation, like predators on carrion.

Soon enough, the midwestern businessmen returned home, and the two men in Cedar Rapids . . .

". . . some very prominent names in the community," Gilhooley said.

"Started their own Circle of Six?" I finished.

"Exactly," he said.

"But they couldn't take a girl from Cedar Rapids because she'd be missed, so they went to the Indian settlement and—"

"That's what the old newspaperman tells me, anyway. There was a police matron named Anna Tolan—she was pretty much like a police officer except nobody wanted to call her that—and she figured the whole thing out about The Circle. And about the murder."

"What murder?"

"In 1903, my friend. A very beautiful young Indian girl of sixteen years was found dead with her nose cut off."

"Who killed her?"

"He says he doesn't know, but that this Anna Tolan sure investigated the case."

"The Indian girl was sixteen," I mused. "They didn't take very young girls, then?"

"No. What they did was to take a girl, and get her addicted to cocaine. Once they'd turned her into an addict, she wasn't ever going to run off. It worked out fine."

"So after this particular girl was killed—"

Gilhooley leered. "After she was killed, and after Anna Tolan started pushing hard for a serious investigation, the businessmen dissolved The Circle of Six and burned down the house they'd built to have all their fun in."

I thought of the ancient mansion where the dog had brought me the arm of the dead woman. That must have been the headquarters of the local Circle of Six in olden times.

"Any of this make sense?"

"Makes a lot of sense," I said, thinking of the dead sisters and why they'd had to die.

"So, you think she'll go out with me?"

"Huh?" I was caught up in my own thoughts. "Who?"

"Kristin."

"Boy, I don't know, Gilhooley."

"I think she was just playing hard to get."

"She was doing a very good job of it."

Then he seemed to ponder something for a long moment. "I wonder if she knows anything about Mao. You reckon?"

"Oh yeah," I said. "She probably sits home every night in her bunny-jammies reading up on the Cultural Revolution."

He laughed. "Man, wouldn't that be great, a cute-lookin' chick like that who digs Mao?"

I guess we each have our own individual fantasies about women.

EIGHT

I had to wait twenty minutes—impatient minutes now that I was beginning to see the shape of all this—before an obliging car appeared and buzzed open the gates. I followed right behind him.

As I pulled my car into an available space, I started wondering how I was going to get up to the second floor to talk to Linda Prine. But there was no problem. As I crossed the lot to the twin buildings, I saw her on the veranda watching me, taking the last of the summer sun, like a vampire draining the last drops of blood from a victim.

She wore a pink string bikini that looked festive against the dusky beauty of her skin, her small breasts eminently edible exotic fruits, her stomach flat and hard—the fierce machismo of female beauty these days. Actually, I've never minded a little extra weight on women, particularly, I suppose, as I get older and have a little extra weight of my own to contend with.

When I got close enough so that she could lean over and speak in a soft voice, and not give her wealthy neighbors the impression that she was Indian trash, she hissed down to me: "This time I'm going to call Perry and I'm not going to stop him from beating you up."

"You do that. You call Perry. I've been looking for him— so have several other people, including his wife." I saw the lie in her glistening eyes, that she could summon him at will. "And you've been looking for him, too, I'll bet. Did he leave you without any spending money?"

"I'm going in now," she told me.

She minced over to the chair she'd been sitting in, picked up her drink and her paperback, and started inside, her mules clacking on the veranda floor. Then she disappeared, the angle of the balcony floor above me cutting her from sight abruptly.

It was time to say it. I called up: "I want to talk to you about your brother. David Rhodes."

The heel-clacking stopped.

I was aware of my surroundings suddenly. Parking lot. 4 P.M. Voice and music at tolerable levels coming from various balconies and open windows. Smell of fading heat and gasoline fumes from cars and trucks on First Avenue. Maintenance man in far corner cursing Lawn-Boy he couldn't get started.

Heels clacking again but a different rhythm this time. No longer sharp, angry. Slow now. A certain weariness in the sound.

She appeared again on the balcony above me. She'd thrown a towel over her shoulders, as if she were not only aware of her near-nakedness but ashamed of it now.

"You bastard."

"We need to talk."

"You bastard. You bastard."

Not until this moment did I realize that she was coked up.

Or coked down, actually—that long dark chill slide into the need for white powder again.

"You bastard," she said one more time. This time she was crying.

A few minutes later, she buzzed me in.

"The two sisters stole you from the reservation when you were six years old. They took you with them when they traveled with the rodeo so you never saw Iowa again until you were a teenager. They also turned you into a junkie so that you'd be more obliging. They started selling you when you were thirteen or fourteen—at least, that's how these things usually go—then when they moved back to Cedar Rapids and got to know all the young high-rollers downtown, they decided to peddle you as this very young, innocent girl. You could pass a good four years younger than you were, so you were perfect for The Circle of Six that Perry Heston and Bryce Cook started up. Except there were never Six—there were just the two of them. They wanted a virginal young girl who was totally at their command and the sisters convinced them that that's exactly what you were. It was a very cushy life for a while, wasn't it? They built this fancy house out in the boonies somewhere and put you up in it and everything was going fine—the sisters had taught you all the ways to keep your benefactors happy—until the sisters got greedy and started blackmailing Heston and Cook. And then it all started coming apart, didn't it? They moved you out of the house to this nice new condo here. They didn't want The Circle of Six anymore but they did want you. They were both in love with you—or addicted to you, anyway. And so they put you here. And then one or both of them killed the sisters. And tried to hang it on David who you'd learned by then was your brother, right?"

Through the open windows you could smell charcoal and burning meat. Men and women in chef hats and aprons with funny sayings on them were grilling steaks and gulping wine from coolers and listening to the crickets and cats and dogs gathering together for their dusk symphony that would be coming up soon.

She wasn't having any steaks or wine. She was having cocaine, a line of it on a small mirror. She snorted it up in an astonishingly delicate and feminine way. She still wore the pink string bikini but now had a blue summer-weight blanket around her. She looked younger and more vulnerable than ever.

"I just can't believe they'd kill anybody," she said, now that cocaine had made her right and whole and strong again. "I really can't. I mean, Bryce has a bad temper, sure, but . . ." She shook her head.

"How did you meet David?"

"In a bar, out at one of the malls. He was a big cruiser, David was. Always hustling. He was a great-looking guy. A lot of white women, really attractive white women, dug that he was a full-blooded Indian. Gave him a real edge of danger, you know what I'm saying?"

"You didn't know he was your brother?"

"No, of course not. How would I? I was just a little girl the last time I'd seen him."

"And he didn't guess your real relationship, either?"

She looked at me. "I know what you want me to say so I'll say it. We had an affair for a while—I'd never been with anybody else since the sisters brought me to Bryce and Perry—and everything was all right until the sisters found out and told me who I really was . . . and who David really was. That's why he killed himself. He couldn't handle what we'd done. He was in love with me . . . and then he found out I was his little sister. No, he just couldn't handle it. His drinking got worse and worse and he started coming around here and making scenes and that's why Bryce and Perry beat him up at the casino. And getting beaten up that way—it all just started coming apart for him. He started following Bryce and Perry around. That's how he found out about that old burned-down mansion. He went out there that night you trailed him to check it out for himself." She shook her head.

"It just all came down for him. He couldn't stand to live anymore."

"How are you handling it?" I said.

"About David and me?" She made a small sad face. "The way the sisters brought me up, I guess I don't get too excited about things like that. But I miss him. He had his demons but he was a good man."

"Like Perry and Bryce are good men?"

She touched a finger to a perfect nostril. She was quick and clean as a cat and even the merest gesture was charged with erotic possibilities. "You make a lot of judgements about people."

"I suppose I do. You were sixteen when Cook and Heston took you."

"You forget. I was supposed to be sixteen but I was actually twenty."

"I guess I was wrong about them. They're a couple of swells."

"They're not as bad as you might think. At first it was just about sex and I didn't like them much, but then later on they fell in love with me—both of them—and they kind of competed against each other. And it was fun to watch. They never hurt me. They never even made me do much sex against my will. Early on I guess they did, wanting to be macho and all, I suppose. But later . . . You're kind of square, Mr. Payne. And you judge everybody by that same square standard. Maybe it's time you looked around."

And then the blood came boiling out of her nose. She must have felt it starting a minute or so earlier when she put the finger to her nostril.

"Shit!" she screamed and kicked off her mules and got up and ran through the condo into the bathroom.

I knew she wouldn't want me to follow. She had an animal's sense of privacy.

She came back a few minutes later and said, "Sometimes the nose gets kind of bad."

"Maybe it's time to think about kicking."

."Maybe you were a priest in a former life."

I looked around the nicely appointed condo. "I think it's coming to an end, Linda."

She sat on the edge of the couch. The blanket was gone. She was mostly naked again. She was amused that I couldn't quit watching her breasts and legs.

"I need to know where the house is."

"What house?"

"You know what house. The house Perry and Bryce built for you."

"Why does it matter? I live here now. They don't even go there much anymore."

"Where is it?"

"You think something happened to them?"

I nodded. "Nobody's seen them for two days. There's a strong possibility that something's happened to them."

"God." She stared out the window.

A sunset that crushed my heart with its melancholy filled the veranda doors.

"Linda."

"I don't know what the fuck I'll do if they're dead or anything." She still stared out the window.

"That's why you've got to tell me where the house is."

"I wouldn't want to start hooking. AIDS scares the hell out of me. I know this Indian girl from Denver, she had AIDS and man, I've never seen anything like it."

She was in some kind of coke reverie. I didn't have the time to walk all the way through it with her.

I got up and went over and touched her bare shoulder. It was my afternoon for shoulders. I got a different kind of erotic charge from this one. Pure sex, no grace notes of house-wifely remorse or suburban angst as with Evelyn Cook. Pure sex.

"You want to fuck or something?" she said looking up at me.

I was startled to find that she was serious and probably not out of any desire for me but because she didn't know what else to do.

"I'm flattered but no, thanks. Right now all I want is that address."

"What am I going to do if they're dead?"

I gave her an Oprah line. "You're young and bright, you can turn your life around."

"That's the trouble."

"What is?"

"I don't want to turn my life around. I like it just the way it is."

Then she told me how and where I could find the house Perry and Bryce had built for her.

———◆———

The red man knew one truth above all others—that he would never be treated as an equal by the white man. For this reason, between 1900–1917, more than twenty-five Indians condemned to be executed took their own lives—a gesture of contempt. They would rather take them than have the white man take them.
                    Professor David Cromwell's Indian Journal

"He told me what happened," Anna said to the Chief twenty minutes after leaving the hospital. "Right there on his death-bed."

"It's his word against Ashlock's, Anna, and guess who this community would believe?"

"But they're going to execute an innocent man."

The sixth of January was the date.

"He isn't an innocent man, Anna. He's the killer. Everything I've learned as a lawman tells me that."

But she could see his doubts in the sad grave gaze and the whiskey bottle he now took from his desk.

"We can't let him be hanged, Chief," Anna said. "We just can't."

NINE

By the time I picked up Cindy, by the time we reached the marina, full night had fallen.

"Everything's put up for the night, sorry," the angular, bald man in the grease-spotted overalls said. "Even the canoes."

The marina was small and hidden behind a stand of cedars. There was a glassed-in area where customers could look at a few new boats and motors and a repair area that smelled of oil. The lights were on in the garage and engines lay on the floor open and stripped, like wounded soldiers. A radio playing an old rhythm and blues song sounded lonely and isolated.

Cindy couldn't stay still. On the way over I'd told her what I'd learned and now that she knew David hadn't killed the sisters, she wanted vengeance. She wanted the killer.

"Would you give us a boat if I doubled your fee?" she asked the man, and disappeared around the far side of the garage.

"I got 'em all put up tonight." His voice said wife and kids and home and relaxation after a hard day. I didn't blame him.

Cindy came back around the corner. "You want to come here a minute?"

The marine man looked at me and frowned, knowing she'd found some way to ruin his night.

I followed him to the far side of the garage.

On a strip of dusty gravel sat a green rowboat with a two-cylinder engine inside. It needed paint.

"You haven't put this away for the night," she said. "How about letting us take it?"

"I'd still have to wait for you to get back and then put it away."

She knew just what to do. She wore a white shirt, a narrow-cut woman's sport jacket and jeans. From the jacket she produced her wallet and from her wallet her badge. It was too dark for him to get a good look at it—to see that she wasn't a Cedar Rapids cop—so, as a good citizen, he was immediately cowed.

"Oh," he said, "a cop."

"You can go on home," she said reassuringly. "I'll throw a tarpaulin over it when we get back."

But he was beginning to have doubts.

"First problem is," he said, "how come you don't use one of the police boats?"

"We're in kind of a hurry and this is kind of a special assignment."

"All right, second question is, do you know anything about gas hoses or hose clamps?"

"I can handle that."

"Don't be too sure. Hose keeps slippin' off."

"We'll be fine," Cindy said.

"You tarp it up when you bring it back—the boat, I mean," he said.

"We'll tarp it up," I said.

"There's a side door, I'll leave it unlocked. You put the motor in there."

"Great."

Five minutes later, we put the rowboat into the water.

Black river surface. Choppy. Touched by starlight. Engine sound harsh and rackety in the gloom. Shouting at each other to be heard. Cold. Goosebump cold. Not dressed for this, either one of us. Black dirty water in small waves and spray all over the boat and our faces and hands. More goosebumps.

Long bend of river. Sandy beaches eastward. Deep forest to the right.

He hadn't been exaggerating about the gasoline hose. It slipped out so badly, the engine shutting down to one cylinder when it did, or shutting off entirely, that we divided up tasks. She steered the boat while I held the hose in place.

Twenty minutes it took for the island to come into view. Perry and Bryce had wanted to build an eyrie and they had succeeded. Behind the scrub pines, in the middle of a grassy island perhaps a half-mile in length, sat a Spanish-style house with a gabled roof. Red tiles and white stucco shone behind a thin shaggy stand of trees. All the windows were dark.

"Maybe they're not here," Cindy shouted above the roar of the engines.

"Maybe not," I shouted back.

As we came up to the beach, I cut the engine. At first, the silence seemed vast and overwhelming. Then small sounds intervened. The river lapping, lapping. Nightbirds crying. Faint, and far off, a tug of some kind, hooting. Fog had settled on the island and played like ghosts among the scrub pines.

The first shot came just as we were dragging the rowboat up on the sandy beach.

The bullet spanged off the motor.

We both dove for the sand.

Fear and anger; fear and anger. I eased the Ruger from my holster. Cindy's Smith & Wesson was already in her hand.

"Bastards," she said.

Suddenly I was covered in cold sweat. My armpits and the soles of my feet were soaked.

"Bastards," she said again.

Two more quick shots kept us flat on the wet sand. From the report, it was easy to tell that the shooter was using a high-powered rifle and that he knew what he was doing. He couldn't pick us off easily in the darkness this way, but he could keep us pinned down until we did something stupid or impulsive.

"Give him a few shots," I whispered.

She lay beside me now, close enough that I could hear her heart pounding through the flesh of her arm and cloth of her sport jacket.

"I'll try to get into the woods over there," I hissed.

"He's a pretty damned good shot."

"I noticed that."

She put four straight shots into the approximate area where the marksman was situated. I took the opportunity to run in zig-zag fashion, almost tripping once in the heavy sand, finally diving for the woods and protection.

By then the shooter had figured out what was going on and was firing at me.

I stayed on the ground until everything was quiet again. Minty-smelling leaves; the odor of summer mud; moonlight dappling the tops of the forest trees. And my own breathing, loud.

I moved in a south-westerly direction, staying on my haunches whenever possible.

Cindy opened up on him again, twice. I heard him swear—I was getting close enough—harsh and masculine. Fear and anger.

I crawled through mud, sand, undergrowth. I snaked through pine, bramble, rasping grasping weed. I crept through shifting shadows of ever-darkening night. Sweat stung and blinded me. But most of the time, thorn and rock and branch tearing my palms and arms and face, I kept moving forward.

I came to the edge of a clearing and saw him on the opposite side, crouched by a large rock at the mouth of a trail leading deep into the forest. From here, he could see the shore, and fire at will. Perry Heston.

I stood up, knees cracking, long thigh muscles and back very sore.

I planed to move around the edge of the small clearing and come up on the other side of him, not give him any chance for a shot at me at all.

I was ready to move when I saw, from the woods directly behind Heston, a lumbering monster of some kind emerging; its facial features were lost in blood and its otherwise white arms glistened with even fresher blood.

"You sonofabitch!" the monster shouted, and it fired twice at Heston.

But Bryce Cook had been injured too badly to shoot straight. His wild shooting gave Heston time to turn around, roll over, and get a good aim of his own.

He put two quick rifle bullets directly into Bryce Cook's chest. Cook didn't so much as teeter, not at first. He stood in the moonlight, white golf shirt and chinos soaked with his own blood, and gazed slowly up at the sky. He looked sad and baffled, a big forlorn animal about to cross over to the Other Side. He collapsed then, without any fuss at all.

"Put the rifle down, Heston," I said.

He hadn't seen me till this moment, but he didn't seem startled or surprised. He simply gave me his best boardroom smirk. "Mr. Payne, I believe."

"You just murdered your best friend."

"Hardly murder. He fired first, you know damned well he did."

"You still didn't have to kill him."

"You're wrong. He tried to shoot me about an hour ago. He was a terrible shot, poor bastard. So I shot him in the shoulder. That's where all the blood came from. The second time he tried to kill me—well, I wasn't so forgiving."

The shot forced Heston to throw himself to the ground.

Cindy came out of the woods.

She walked over to him. Before he had a chance to get to

his feet, she kicked him viciously in the ribs. I could hear bone crack. Then she kicked him in the face, and more bone cracked.

He cursed her and tried not to cry but it wasn't easy, especially when she caught him in the ribs again.

I went over and took her arm. ''C'mon, you've had your fun.''

She looked dazed as Bryce Cook had, there at the last, all feeling focused on a single goal—destruction.

Wind came up then, cold and pocked with sprinkles of rain; the fog wound, snake-like, around the shaggy pines. I looked over at the house. A light had come on in a second-floor room. A silhouette moved behind sheer curtains.

His ribs were broken and it wasn't easy for him to get to his feet, yet neither of us helped him. We just watched. He still had an air of command about him, that was the strange thing. Some part of this man could never be broken, as hundreds of business rivals had no doubt learned.

''I want you to know something, Payne.''

''Know what?''

''Those two sisters?''

''Yes.''

''I killed them.''

''Why?''

''Because they were blackmailing me.''

''They'd been blackmailing you for two years. Why kill them now?''

''Because I got tired of it.''

''Just all of a sudden?''

''Just all of a sudden.''

Cindy said, ''You tried to make the police think my husband did it.'' She took a step forward again. She wanted one more poke at him. Not that I blamed her.

I pointed to the house. ''Who's in there?''

''Nobody,'' Heston said. He was groaning again. His face was filthy with blood. His nose was broken. I took out my handkerchief and tossed it to him. It fell at his feet. He had to bend over to get it and the action made him stifle a scream.

"Bullshit. A light just went on."

"They're on automatic timers." His voice was a croak of pain. "In case of prowlers."

"Right," I said to Cindy. "How about you keep him here and I go up there?"

"I can't guarantee I won't hurt him some more."

I smiled. "Well, I guess there's no way I can stop you if I'm not here, is there?"

I went up to the house.

Among white policemen, it was generally acknowledged that if most of your homicide victims were red or black, your career was in serious trouble.
                    Professor David Cromwell's Indian Journal

Hvacek lived until December 6, but he never regained full consciousness so Anna could question him no more.

She did, however, write down everything she knew in a letter and mailed it to Douglas Ashlock. She advised him against enlisting the help of either the Mayor or the Chief, otherwise she would be forced to make her letter public.

On the night of December 10, Douglas Ashlock stood outside the police station, which was located in the downstairs of a hotel, and waited for Anna to appear.

The town was decorated for Christmas. Wreaths, bells, paintings of Santa Claus were everywhere. A light snow had begun falling along with night.

Anna came out just after 6:00 P.M., bundled up for the freezing weather. She was startled to see Ashlock.

"I wondered if I could walk you home, Officer Tolan?"

"All right."

They began walking.

"I got your letter."

"I assumed that's why you were here."

"And I've done some checking up on you."

She looked over at him. "Going to try and sully my name in some way?"

"On the contrary. I'm going to make you a rich woman."

"Oh?"

"Yes. I've had my lawyer give you more than twenty thousand shares in my most prosperous company. You can sell the stock now for a small fortune, or hold on to it and make even more eventually. At least that's my opinion."

"And all I have to do for this is to—what?"

"Forget about Tall Tree."

"He's innocent."

"So you say."

"You know he's innocent."

"Do I, Officer Tolan?"

They walked on. The street lamps gave the white snow a buttery glow.

"Do you have any idea how much money I'm offering you, Officer Tolan?"

"I'm more concerned with Tall Tree."

"I'm offering you a great deal of money, Officer Tolan. A very great deal."

She started walking away from him, then, and very quickly, as if he were contaminated.

"I don't want your money, Mr. Ashlock," she called over her shoulder as she headed into the darkness between street lamps. "I just want you to tell the truth."

TEN

The front door was ajar. I put out my hand to push through and noticed the bloody handprint on the edge of the stucco doorway. Still glistening. Bryce Cook's, no doubt.

The downstairs was chill and dark. Long-ago fires in the fireplace smelled woody and warm. The shape and slant of the stairway was outlined in the shadows.

I crossed the vestibule to the steps and that was when I heard something crash upstairs. And then a curse: female.

I went up the stairs slowly. When I reached the landing, I looked right and saw nothing but the deep darkness. To the left, however, and far down the narrow hall, burned an electric lamp dim as a guttering candle.

I took out my Ruger. I went on tiptoe, closer, closer to the faint light, waiting for some crashing sound to startle me again.

I pressed flat on the far side of the lighted doorway, Ruger ready. I said, "I'd like to talk to you, Mrs. Heston."

Silence.

"Did you hear me, Mrs. Heston?"

Clank of bottle-neck on drinking glass.

"Mrs. Heston?"

"How did you figure it out, Mr. Payne? How did you know that I killed those two women?"

"I remembered those library books in the back of your car," I said. "One of them was *True Crimes*, volume two. I looked it up at the library and found a story on Native American mutilations. Then I ran some statistics on the computer about copycat killings. Sometimes the police put out false information to trap copycats. That's what they did in the case you copied. The information about cutting off their arms was false. But you didn't know that."

"No," she said. "That's not how you knew. You have kind eyes, Mr. Payne, and can see into people's souls, and you saw into mine and that's how you knew I killed those two women."

"I'd like to come in now."

Quick sad laugh. "Are you afraid I'm going to shoot you?"

"Your husband wants me to believe he killed those two women."

"Should that make me think of him as noble, Mr. Payne?"

"No. But I thought you should know."

"He did just what my great-great-grandfather did. Disgraced the family with his whoring around. It would've all come out—how those two sisters stole the little girl, and how my husband and Bryce built this place just as The Circle of Six built theirs one hundred years ago—and then what?"

Clank of bottle-neck on glass again.

"I have a sense of propriety, Mr. Payne, of dignity."

She was pretty drunk and I felt sorry for her.

"People always say he made my family name important

again, Mr. Payne—but only with money. I restored the dignity. All the work I've done over the years—and people said it was all him. And then he built this place and brought that Indian whore here and—. But I shouldn't hate her, should I?''

"I don't think so.''

She hiccoughed. It wasn't funny; it was sad.

"I'd like to come in and talk to you,'' I said.

"I look like shit.''

"So do I.''

This time there was some gentleness in her laugh. "I really do like you, Payne.'' Then, "I have a gun. I shot Bryce with it. I wanted to shoot my husband, too, but he got away.'' Pause. "And I'm drinking again. Four different times at the clinic and I'm drinking again.''

"You know what I'd like to do?''

"What?''

"Come in and have a drink with you.''

Pause. "You want me to give you the gun, don't you?''

"I promise I won't try to take it away. If you want to give it to me, fine. If you don't, fine. We'll just have a drink.''

"Oh shit, Payne, it's just all so confusing and when I wake up tomorrow—. Oh God, I won't be able to face it. Any of it. They gave me electro-shock six times, did I tell you that?''

"No, I guess you didn't.''

"'Riding the lightning' is what the regulars called it. I rode the lightning. I loved it. That was the awful thing. Everybody else who got it hated it but I loved it because it made me forget.''

"I'd really like to come in and have a drink.''

"I was never unfaithful to him, even when I had a chance.''

"You're not the kind. You're a good woman.''

Then she was crying. "It's so bad when you wake up and you can't quite remember anything. That's how I'll be tomorrow—I'll be so scared . . . Can you get me help, Payne?''

"Yes. Yes, I can.''

And then she did it.

Pulled the trigger. I was through the door in moments, running the length of a long den with fireplace and built-in book-cases.

She sat in an important leather chair, the sort that many generations of tycoons have favored.

The gun was still in her hand.

I raised my eyes and saw the hole she'd put in the wall behind her.

"I've never, never been able to do it, Payne. I just don't have the guts. I've tried but I just can't go through with it."

She had aged many years since the last time I'd seen her, a sorrowful aging of the eyes especially. And some madness, too. Definitely some madness.

Her left hand lay delicately on the breast of her white blouse; her right offered the gun for me to take. It was a Walther P-5, very big for her small hand. "This is Bryce's gun," she said.

As I hefted the gun in my hand and slipped it into the pocket of my sport coat, she raised her eyes to me. "It's over now, isn't it, Payne?"

"Yes, it's over now."

"I don't know why he would have done such a thing. I gave him a name that was so important to protect."

She started crying.

"I suppose it's silly, isn't it, about the name?"

"No, it isn't silly at all."

"Would you hold me, Payne? I'm so scared. I feel like I'm a little girl."

She stood up and I took her in my arms and held her. She put her warm face into my neck and sobbed. Her knees began to shake and I was afraid she might slip to the floor so I lifted her and carried her back to the important leather chair and she sat in my lap and cried in the island silence and island darkness.

I wasn't sure what she was crying about now—many, many things, I suspected—or whether I should try to talk to her or not.

She said, "I used to sit in my father's lap this way." She leaned her face away from my shoulder so I could see her. "I loved my father very much."

"Yes; you told me that once."

"I have to be strong now, don't I, Payne?"

"Very strong."

"Do you think I can handle it?"

"Yes."

"Maybe I'll surprise myself."

"Maybe you will."

"Will you call the police now and get it all started?"

"Yes."

"I'd appreciate it."

She got up. It was an awkward moment, like high-school necking when the parents suddenly turn on a light. She made a fuss of straightening her blouse and dark slacks.

There was a wide desk. I walked to it and dialed the Cedar Rapids police.

I asked for the Detective Bureau and drew a cop named Ferguson. When I told him what had happened, and when he realized the social status of the people involved, he said, "Holy shit."

I looked back at the beautiful ruined woman.

"Yeah," I said into the phone. "Holy shit."

———◆———

Colonel Richard Greaves often talked about teaching one of his Indian guides new words. When Greaves taught him "inexorable," the guide said, "The white man murdering us was inexorable." Greaves laughed but the Indian did not.

Professor David Cromwell's Indian Journal

But to no avail did Anna Tolan work to convince Chief Ryan that he should go to the Mayor with her theories.

Christmas came, and went.

Three days before the execution was scheduled, the worst blizzard of the new century struck. Cedar Rapids was basically shut down. Even some trains were stopped.

*   *   *

On the third day of the blizzard, just as she was about to
leave the police station for her morning rounds, a newspaperman, bundled up as a mummy, came in the front door and
said, "Did you hear about Doug Ashlock?"

Several officers, Anna included, turned to the newspaperman immediately.

"Had some kind of breakdown. They're puttin' him in the
bug-house upstate. Apparently he just broke down completely."

"When did they take him?" Anna asked.

"Early this morning. The servants said they've never seen
nothin' like it."

Forty minutes later, Anna was admitted into the Ashlock mansion.

A servant led her into the den where Mrs. Ashlock, a fetching auburn-haired lady in a silk and organdy dress stood looking out the window at the falling snow.

She turned and said to the servant, "Please close the door,
Samuel."

"Yes, ma'am." Samuel closed the door.

Mrs. Ashlock—Eleanor to her friends—then did a most
unexpected thing. She crossed the room to where Anna stood.
And slapped her hard across the face.

"I'm glad you came. You're the reason my husband had
his breakdown. You and your constant pestering."

"He killed that woman."

"No," Eleanor Ashlock said. "He did not."

From the pocket of her dress, she took a sheet of paper
that looked familiar. "This is the letter you sent my husband,
along with your 'list of evidence' as you called it." She
waved the letter angrily in Anna's face. "You're right, he
was at the murder scene and he *did* drop his black moon
lure—but he got there too late. Somebody had already murdered the Indian girl—somebody whose reputation in this
town among the respectable people would be ruined utterly
and forever."

Once more, she waved Anna's letter in her face.

"You misread your evidence, Miss Tolan. A tortoiseshell comb. A button to a *woman's* dress. Shoeprints from a *woman's* shoe. And the Indian girl's wounds were light—far less than a man would make them."

Now Anna realized what she was hearing—a confession.

Eleanor Ashlock smiled. "But there's nothing you can do about it, Miss Tolan. Not anything at all."

Anna tried to speak but Eleanor Ashlock raised her voice and said, "Samuel!"

The servant reappeared instantly. Stayed at the door.

"Show Miss Tolan out, Samuel."

"Yes, ma'am."

But Anna would not be moved without her say. "I won't let you get away with it, Mrs. Ashlock. I'm going to tell the Chief and the Mayor and anybody else who'll listen to the truth—and I'll make them believe me."

But all Eleanor Ashlock said was, "I told you to show her out, Samuel."

"Yes, ma'am."

Anna glared at the woman one more time and then followed the servant out.

The Chief couldn't refuse Anna. She wouldn't let him. He got the Mayor over and the County Attorney and a representative from the prison. Over the course of the next twenty-four hours, they had four meetings. Anna was at each one, telling her story over and over.

"Do you know who you're accusing of murder?" the Mayor said.

"Yes, sir, I do."

"And do you have any proof of this?"

"Yes, sir, I do."

"Other than this 'scientific detection' of yours, I mean?"

"Well, sir, I guess not."

"Well, then, let's forget this whole damned thing. If you think I'm going to stand by and see you accuse one of the finest women in this town of—"

The County Attorney looked at the Chief and said, "I'm

very busy, Chief. I need to get back to my office.'' He gave Anna a scornful glance. ''As far as I'm concerned, this has all been a waste of time.''

The Mayor, too, picked up his hat and left.

''He's innocent,'' Anna said when she was alone with the Chief.

''Anna, this is so preposterous. That Mrs. Ashlock would—''

''She did it.''

''You have no proof whatsoever.''

''Her word.''

''Her word? You told me yourself she said you could never prove it.''

Anna didn't make a ceremony of it. Simply put her badge on the desk. ''I'm resigning, Chief.''

''Anna, listen, please—''

She shook her head. ''I know what you're up against, Chief. And I know there's nothing you can do. I mean, I really don't have any evidence.''

''Anna, I just wish you'd be sensible . . .''

In the morning, she took the train to Des Moines and visited the Governor. He was a friendly, plump man who wore a brocaded vest and a bright yellow cravat.

''Do you have any proof of your accusations?''

''Not what you'd call proof, no.''

''Yet you'd expect me to call off the execution?''

''Just postpone it.''

''He was found guilty, young woman. Aren't you aware of that?''

''Yes, I am.''

''And he was allowed an appeal. Are you also aware of that?''

''Yes, I am.''

''He's been given every opportunity.''

''He's not guilty.''

''You say.''

''Yes, sir, I say.''

"I'm sorry, young woman, there just isn't anything I can do to help you."

Anna nodded. She thought for a moment of saying something dramatic—some accusation against the justice system—but suddenly she felt very, very weary.

On the morning of January 6, at exactly 6:00 A.M., in the cold stone shadowy room where such things took place, Tall Tree was hanged by the neck until he was pronounced dead.

At the time, Anna was in the back pew of a Catholic church, attending early mass.

It was raining when she got out but she didn't notice it. She knew where she was going and what she was going to do. A little rain wasn't going to deter her.

"Why, Anna," Mrs. Wydmore said. "What're you doing out so early?"

"I just wondered if Trace was up yet."

"I think so. I mean, he should be. He's got to go to the office pretty soon."

"I wondered if I could see him a moment."

She hadn't seen Mrs. Wydmore since Trace's engagement had been officially announced.

"Of course," Mrs. Wydmore said.

She put Anna in the parlor and then went looking for her son in the vast and well-appointed house.

Trace appeared a few minutes later. His hair was slicked down, a clean white celluloid collar rode his clean white shirt, and he looked absolutely mystified as to what she was doing here.

"Hi, Anna. Nice to see you again."

"Nice to see you, Trace."

"Any special reason you're here this morning?"

"I wanted to ask you a question."

"Oh?"

"I wanted to ask you if you'd marry me."

They were married six months later. Three nights before the wedding, Anna gave herself to Trace. She never once regretted it.

ELEVEN

Two days later, on a sunny morning when the horses ran in the hills and the harvest was underway in the fields, I got the biplane fired up and ready to fly back home. There was a peace that only the sky could give me, a peace that would do for me what Claire Heston had said "riding the lightning" had done for her—made her forget. Long and sapping the months had been, from that first fight behind the casino to the impudent news coverage of Claire Heston's murders and suicide, as if truth were as simple as facts.

I was just putting on my helmet when I heard a car horn honk.

A white Ford police car was trailing rusty dust in the late-morning sunlight, coming fast on the gravel road that led to this tiny private airport.

I saw immediately who was driving and I wondered if she'd be any friendlier these days. After Perry Heston had been taken to the hospital to be treated for shock—County Attorney charges to be determined later—Cindy had acted as cold and hostile as she had after David took his life.

Then I saw the three old people in the back seat—Iron Crow and Silver Moon and their friend Lone Tree.

The Ford bumped and bounced across the grass and pulled up close to the tail of the plane.

Cindy, in crisp khaki uniform, killed the engine, hopped out, helped the three older people out and then beckoned for me to come over.

But as I started walking toward her, she left the others and walked toward me, too.

"I wanted to thank you."

"No need," I said.

"I was kind of a bitch again, wasn't I?"

I smiled. "Kind of, I guess."

"I wish I had PMS. Maybe I could explain my dark side that way."

She touched my arm lightly. "When I saw Claire Heston there . . . All I could think of was David. You know, the two of them." She squinted in the sunlight. "I wish I was better at explaining myself."

"You're doing fine."

"So you'll accept my apology?"

"Hell yes, why wouldn't I?"

Then she leaned forward and kissed me on the cheek. "I had fun that night. I mean, we actually fit together pretty well, don't we?"

"You noticed that, too, huh?"

We looked at each other a long moment and then she said, "Lone Tree, their friend who's terrified of flying . . ."

"Yeah?"

"She wants to give it a try. You have time?"

''Why not?''

''You'll really have to go easy, Payne. She's more scared than Iron Crow and Silver Moon were put together.''

''I'll treat her like she was my own grandmother.''

She grinned and slid her arm around my waist. It felt good there, warm and strong and friendly.

I took Lone Tree up that morning, and indeed treated her very much the way I would have my own grandmother, and then I fired up the bird for myself and was off.

For a time I thought of Claire and David and the two hard-scrabble Indian sisters who'd kidnapped Linda Prine.

But then I didn't think of any of it because the clouds were sufficient unto my needs, as was the sun and wind and sky, and the rolling land of Iowa below.

BIBLIOGRAPHY

Richard Bach: *Bi-Plane* (Harper & Row, 1966)

François Barret-Ducrocq: *Love in the Time of Victoria* (New Left Books, 1991)

Mary Bennett: *An Iowa Album* (The University of Iowa Press, 1990)

Mary Brave Bird: *Ohitika Bird* (Grove Press, 1993)

Tom C. Cooper, ed.: *Iowa's Natural Heritage* (Iowa Natural Heritage Foundation, 1982)

Edith Rule: *True Tales of Iowa* (Yelland & Haynes, 1932)

David Rasdal, *Cedar Rapids Gazette* columnist, wrote three columns on Native American casinos that were very helpful.

Here is an excerpt from *Harlot's Moon*, the new, chilling novel from Ed Gorman:

The room was dark and tomb-cold. The only light came from the bathroom in the back. There was a mixture of smells: mildew, dirty rugs, towels, linen, and death. The dead man had shit himself. He lay hunched fetus-style in the middle of the double bed. He was without shirt or socks. His pants were unbuckled. I wasn't sure what to make of any of these details. His mouth was open as if in a silent scream, the lips violent red with blood.

I stood in the room and let myself be suffused with its history, all the betrayals and loneliness. The furnishings, stained, chipped, and dusty, looked too dirty to sit on.

"What's his name, Steve?"

"Father Daly. Peter Daly."

"From St. Mallory's?"

"Yes."

I took a penlight from my sport jacket and knelt down next to the bed. I wanted a closer look at the wound in the chest. It was a large one. I suspected he'd been stabbed several times in the heart. But his open mouth was even more perplexing. This was not commonly seen in a murder victim. I shone my light inside and gagged. My entire body spasmed. I'd never seen anything like this.

"What is it?" Steve said.

"His tongue has been cut out."

"Oh, my Lord."

I went in the back and looked in the bathroom. Though I saw no blood I smelled some, probably in the dirt- and mustard-colored carpeting. The police lab man would use a test called Luminol to see if there was indeed blood in the rug.

Steve Gray followed me around like a child trailing a parent. He wore a white button-down shirt, a blue windbreaker, chinos and Reeboks. I wondered if the Pope ever dressed like that.

"You looking for anything in particular, Robert?"

"Not really," I said.

When I came out of the bathroom, he said, "We need to talk."

I shook my head. "Talk is for later. What we need to do

now is call the police. You can't afford to stall them any longer.''

"I called two other people," he said. "And they're on their way over."

"Who are they?"

"Bob Wilson, who is the President of the Parish Board, and Father Ryan. He's the only priest left at St. Mallory's now—besides me, I mean." He stared down at the dead priest. "We don't always agree, Father Ryan and I, but this time we do."

"Why invite them now?"

He raised his gaze from the corpse on the bed.

"They're better at press relations than I am. I'll need their help."

I surveyed chairs, end-tables, bed and bathroom counters for anything that had been left behind. There was a golden earring on one of the end-tables. It had been cast in the shape of a heart. I left it where it was. The lab folks would be very angry if I didn't. An open condom wrapper on the bed proclaimed itself to be of the ribbed variety, with a ''special'' tip.

"Is that what they call a French tickler?" Steve said.

"Uh-huh."

He made a face. "He was quite a guy."

I didn't want to touch the phone so I walked out of the room and went up to the office. Steve walked alongside me.

"The night man here goes to St. Mallory's," he said. "He'd had complaints about some kind of fight going on in the room. When he let himself in and found Father Daly dead, he called me right away."

"What's the night man's name?"

"Paul Gaspard."

"Let's go see him. I'm not sure he did you any favors. The cops're really going to be mad."

"This will hurt the parish," he said, not heeding me. "The scandal. I can hear all the jokes already."

We passed a series of junk cars lined up along the walk. They all had out-of-state plates—Missouri, Wisconsin, Minnesota . . . drifters drifting, desperately trying to find justice or at least shelter from injustice. They'd work minimum wage for a time, maybe enroll their two or three scruffy youngsters in a local school, and then some night they'd do something crazy, or something crazy would be done to them, and they'd start drifting again. You see the kids sometimes, peering out the back windows of rusty old cars. They can break your heart.

Just before we reached the office, I said, "What was Father Daly doing here?"

"I don't know."

I stopped and looked at him. With his pugged nose and curly dark hair, his face would always look younger than his years.

"You wouldn't lie to me, would you, Steve? I'm trying to help you, remember?"

He looked away from me. Big semis pushed into the sheets of rain marching down the nearby interstate. All the cars had their lights on, fragile prayers in a world of thunder and lightning and darkness.

He turned back to me. "I think he was having an affair."

"Who with?"

His smile was sour, his tone defensive. "Despite what the tabloids have to say about us, most priests have affairs with women, not other men or little children."

Steve hadn't given a name. I decided to ignore that for a while.

"Couldn't he get in trouble for having an affair?"

Steve nodded. "Yes, and especially in this diocese. Bishop Curry doesn't put up with anybody breaking the vow of chastity. He has also been known to turn pedophile priests over to the police. He's a tough guy."

"Was Father Daly a nice guy?"

He shrugged, glanced up at the line of raindrops dripping from the edge of the overhang that kept us dry. Everything smelled cold. Everything looked drab and sad.

"I'm not sure anybody would have called him nice."

"He have any enemies?"

"A couple, as a matter of fact."

"Any idea who they might be?"

"Well," he said, "for starters I'd say the husbands of the two women he had affairs with while he was supposed to be counseling them on their marriages. The husbands weren't at

all happy about that. In fact, one of them was going to sue
Father Daly for alienation of affection.'' He smiled bleakly.
''I guess there are some things we can forgive as priests that
we can't as men. Father Daly caused a lot of trouble in his
time, I'm afraid.''

''I take it you'll tell the police this?''

''I won't have any choice, will I?''

We went inside. When Steve saw the woman behind the
counter, he said, ''Oh, where's Paul?''

''Paul left,'' she said. ''His shift ended twenty minutes
ago.'' She nodded to an ancient dusty wall clock. She was
maybe sixty with dentures that clicked and an angry snarl of
hair that a beautician had tinted an impossible orange. ''Help
you gentlemen?''

''May I use the phone here?''

She pushed a black phone toward me. ''Long as it's local.''

''He's calling the police,'' Steve said. ''There's a dead man
in Room 154.''

''Oh Lord, not another one,'' she said calmly.

''Another one?'' I asked as I dialed.

''Couple years ago they found some hooker with her throat
cut. There must've been cops here for two weeks, traipsing
in and out. Scared the heck out of our customers. I mean, a
lot of them don't want anybody to know they're here.''

I talked to a homicide detective and gave her all the information I had. She said that a black and white would be there
within a matter of minutes, and that she herself would follow
shortly afterwards.

Steve was over by the door. ''Father Ryan and Bob Wilson
just pulled in. I'd better go back to the room.''

''I'll come with you,'' I said. I pushed the phone back.
''Thanks.''

''You know the guy personally?'' the woman asked me.

''Yes,'' Steve said, and I could see the pain it caused him
to say this. ''He was a priest.''

''You're kidding me,'' the woman said. ''A priest!'' Her
dentures clicked and she made a grim face. ''Boy, you just
don't know who to trust these days, do you?''

We walked back to Room 154.

Father Ryan was a tall, slender man with thinning blond hair and thick eyeglasses. He was dressed in priestly black, and a white Roman collar. He had a steel handshake.

Bob Wilson was big, beefy, whiskey-faced, and blustery. He had the air of a good bar-room brawler that his gray business suit, white shirt and blue tie couldn't quite offset. While he was still shaking my hand, he said to Steve Gray, "This is great. We're supposed to start our fund-raising drive next week, Monsignor."

"We'll be all right, Bob, just stay calm," Steve said. I remembered him saying that Wilson and the priest would know how to handle the press. Given his air of frenzy, I wouldn't let Wilson anywhere near the press.

I went over to the door, pushed it open and marched inside. They followed me. We were like teenagers at a carnival, about to gaze upon one of the world's most frightening sights: a murdered man.

"Boy, what did he do?" Bob Wilson said as soon as he was inside. "Crap his pants or what?"

Father Ryan was more solemn. He went over and stood next to the bed and stared down at Father Daly's body.

He reached out a long arm and touched the dead priest's shoulder. Then he closed his eyes and began praying silently.

We all stood in silence until he was finished. I checked out the room with a couple of glances. Everything was as it had been—bathroom light on, door ajar, ashtrays clean, rusty metal wastebasket empty and tipped over on its side, golden earring on end-table, black oxfords and socks near the head of the bed, man's white shirt tossed over the back of a chair.

When he opened his eyes, Father Ryan said, "I got to know his sister pretty well, Monsignor. She's over in Omaha. I can call her if you'd like."

"I'd appreciate that, Father."

Wilson, all angry energy, was stalking around the room.

"What was he doing here, anyway? Cheap motel like this. God Almighty."

Yeah, he'd make a beautiful press spokesman all right.

He started to pick up the ashtray.

"Don't touch anything," I said.

Wilson looked first at Steve and then at me. "Exactly who are you, anyway, Mr. Payne?"

"Robert was an FBI agent for a little over ten years," Steve said. "Now he's a consultant on murder cases to police departments."

Wilson said, "Oh. Sorry I snapped at you then. I guess you know what you're talking about after all."

He walked back to the bathroom. "All right if I pee? I've had three cups of coffee and no breakfast."

"I wish you'd go down to the office, if you wouldn't mind," I said. "The police may find something useful in the toilet bowl."

"What a job," he said, "pawing through toilet bowls."

He left and Steve said, "He's actually a very decent family man."

Before I could say anything, Father Ryan said, "He works very hard for our parish, Mr. Payne. We wouldn't have been able to make any of the church improvements if it hadn't been for Bob Wilson."

Steve was nodding agreement, when the two uniforms came through the door.

They introduced themselves and started the process of securing the crime scene.

"I'm afraid we'll have to ask you to wait outside," the young uniform said. "I understand that they have coffee and rolls down in the office."

I was just turning to go when I glanced over at the end-table where the golden earring had been.

I walked across to the table and looked around at the floor, in case the earring had been knocked off.

But the earring was gone, even though I'd seen it just a few minutes ago.

I looked at Steve, Father Ryan, and Bob Wilson.

Only Bob Wilson had been anywhere near it. Only Bob Wilson could have taken it.

But why was an earring found at the crime scene so important to a good family man like him?

Harlot's Moon—now available in hardcover from
St. Martin's Press!

The scars on her wrists, throat and chest told the story. Somehow Audra Delaney had survived a brutal rape ten years ago, but with her memory of her attacker shattered. Then the unthinkable happens: she hears his voice on the radio, and now all she lives for are dark dreams of revenge.

She was his one loose end—the only one who got away, the only one who can still destroy him. All he has to do is find out her name, so he can silence her forever.

Soon, they're racing neck-and-neck, stalking each other in a world of shadows and evil, where it will take all of Audra's strength and the unexpected ingenuity of a child genius to survive . . .

DEAD EVEN

A gripping novel of psychological terror

EMMA BROOKES